HIDING

HIDING

A NOVEL BY **HENRY TURNER**

CLARION BOOKS
Houghton Mifflin Harcourt
Boston   New York

Clarion Books
3 Park Avenue
New York, New York 10016

Clarion Books is an imprint of Houghton Mifflin Harcourt Publishing Company.

hmhco.com

The text was set in Dante MT Std.

Library of Congress Cataloging-in-Publication Data

Names: Turner, Henry, 1962–author.
Title: Hiding / a novel by Henry Turner.
Description: Boston ; New York : Clarion Books, Houghton Mifflin Harcourt, [2018] | Summary: "When a teen boy who excels at being unseen finds himself hiding in his ex-girlfriend's house, he uncovers carefully concealed truths about her, her family, and himself." — Provided by publisher
Identifiers: LCCN 2017018451 | ISBN 9780544284777 (hardcover)
Subjects: | CYAC: Secrets — Fiction. | Family problems — Fiction. | Dating (Social customs) — Fiction. | Death — Fiction.
Classification: LCC PZ7.1.T877 Hid 2018 | DDC [Fic] — dc23
LC record available at https://lccn.loc.gov/2017018451

Printed in the United States of America
DOC 10 9 8 7 6 5 4 3 2 1
4500701984

For my wife and son

HIDING

CHAPTER
ONE

I'm good at hiding. I think it's what I'm best at. If you're going to believe anything I say, I think you have to know that.

I'm very good at hiding.

I don't just mean hide-and-seek, going in a closet or something. That's just one kind of hiding.

Real hiding happens when everybody can see you, but they don't notice you. That's the real thing.

To do that, you have to be really aware of other people. You have to kind of get to know what sort of people they are to be sure they don't ever look at you, or notice you.

It's kind of hard to understand.

Of course, I find it easy to understand, because I've been hiding all my life.

In one way or another.

It all started when playing games as a little kid. I loved the weird sense of being totally alone behind a bush while whoever I was playing with was out there creeping around trying to find me. I loved watching them look. I felt so safe and protected, like the whole world had gone away, and I thought I never really wanted to be found.

But I no longer need a bush or a closet or a box or some obvious place—what everybody calls a hiding place. I feel I can hide anywhere, even when I'm standing right next to you.

There was a kid in my class who said the teacher always called on him when he didn't know the answer. This was, like, the fourth grade. He was this kid who always sat in class leaning back in his chair really far like it might fall, and sometimes he scratched himself or even picked his nose like nobody else was even around, and these were of course the moments the teacher always chose to single him out.

But he didn't think she called on him because of that stuff, or because he was sort of overweight and had a big fan of frizzy red hair and was definitely the most noticeable kid in class anyways.

She did it, he claimed, to embarrass him and show that he was stupid and just sort of blind to the world, and he thought she got a big kick out of doing it, like it was some sort of game for her.

How she treated him was pretty mean, I'll admit that, but that wasn't what I told him.

I said to him, "Well, there're two ways to deal with that. Study, or learn to hide."

"Hide?" he said. "I wouldn't want to do that."

We were in the cafeteria while we talked, eating lunch, and even then he was leaning back really far in his chair—I can't remember whether he was picking his nose or not.

But I do remember he rolled his eyes and said I was a little nuts.

I couldn't agree with that, so I went on to ask him if he knew why the teacher never called on me, whether I knew the answer or not.

"No," he said.

So I told him.

I said I watched her. I always paid *attention* to her, even if I wasn't looking straight at her. She never saw me drifted off like a sitting duck, waiting to be picked on. She never really saw me at all. I never got so *comfortable* that anybody would ever think I was *blind* to the world, but always stayed really well *aware* of it, and I would sit so still and watch her so calmly that she never noticed me and never thought of singling me out for anything.

I just wasn't there.

For her, at least.

A better example is something I did three months ago

—actually just a little less than three months ago; I mean the end of last May. It happened at this funeral, and it's a perfect example of how I can sometimes walk around and never be seen by anybody.

Now, I call that *hiding* because I can definitely be seen if I want to. But I usually don't want to.

The truth is, I never even meant to go to the funeral at all. I didn't, really. I certainly wasn't *invited* or anything. The thing is that I'd been walking around—it was a Sunday and this was almost three months ago, like I said, and I really never had anything much to do on Sundays anyways, especially right then after school had let out for summer.

I guess I wasn't feeling too good at the time. My girlfriend had just broken up with me. You get the idea. So I was out just sort of wandering, telling myself I was not headed anywhere, when I found myself trudging up the hill from my house, passing this intersection at the top of it, and crossing the street into the next neighborhood, which is, like, the pretty wealthy area, where all the houses are big, and where my girlfriend—my ex-girlfriend—lives.

All I can say is that I never really consciously thought about it or meant to do it, but pretty soon I was hiding in the bushes across the street from her house.

It's not like I *expected* to see her or anything, but I stayed in the bushes awhile, just thinking about her, and other stuff, too, but mainly her, and that's when she came out of the house.

Laura didn't look like herself. That's her name, by the way —Laura. She looked older. Serious and somber. Like a real young woman, not a girl anymore at all.

She looked different than I'd ever seen her.

For one thing, she had on this very sheer black dress that went down to her knees. It shone really brightly against the green grass of her lawn. She didn't usually wear such stuff. Her hair, which fell to her shoulders and is dark brown, shone too, just like the dress. She had a little shawl around her shoulders, black as well. And she had on black shoes with pretty high heels.

She looked beautiful, as usual. Except her face. Her face looked terrible. I don't mean she wasn't pretty anymore. She was always pretty. But she felt sad. I could tell.

More than sad. She felt terrible. I could see it.

Something awful had happened. I didn't know what.

Her mother was there with her. She also wore black. Not Laura's dad—he was off somewhere on business, probably; he always was.

Her brother, Jack, was there, though. Big guy. Football. Stanford, I think. He didn't wear black. I seem to remember he didn't wear any black at all.

They stood there a moment, close together, in front of the very green lawn in front of their house, in relief, almost, because of all the black they had on—except of course for Jack. None of them said anything. It was like they needed to take a moment, or hadn't quite made up their minds about something.

Then they all piled into their car, which was parked on the street, and headed off down the road, with their headlights turned on, even though it was daytime.

I watched the car drive away. But it didn't feel right just to stand there. I had to know why she looked like that. So I came out of the bushes and followed them.

Well, I don't know if *followed* is the right word. Let's just say I walked in the same direction they drove, because it isn't like I could keep up with the car or anything. It was out of sight pretty quickly.

But other cars came by, with their headlights on too.

I knew what that meant. The cars were driving to a funeral.

So every time I saw another car with its headlights on, I just kept walking, and it turned out all I had to do was walk straight about a mile and down a big hill to York Road, which separates the rich area from people who are really pretty poor, but there are businesses and stuff on the street, because York Road is a big wide street in my city, with plenty of businesses and gas stations.

And a funeral parlor.

When I got to York I stood on the corner. Passing traffic blew up clouds of gritty dust from the street. I spotted Laura's car parked on the side street beside the funeral parlor, which was on the corner right across from me. Her car was easy to spot because it was long and black, and everything else was a junker.

All I did was sort of dart across the street, between buses and cars because the traffic was pretty heavy there, always is. I just slipped through, and I'm sure nobody really saw me.

When I was across, I went up the side street and crouched between Laura's car and this beat-up Toyota behind it. I waited a minute, listening, and when it seemed everything was settled inside the funeral home, I went around front.

The window was crowded with flowers. I looked through. I saw a bunch of people with the usual sort of attitudes. I knew the deal; I'd been to a couple funerals before. Some of the people were crying, a couple women, especially. Most were just standing around. It was a closed coffin—I could see that when the crowd parted. I didn't see Laura; she was buried in the crowd. There were more flowers everywhere and the room was white.

Two men in suits came out front and started smoking cigarettes. I turned and acted like I was waiting for a bus, standing behind this pretty thick telephone pole next to the bus-stop sign. I seriously thought the men didn't see me. I'm actually sure they didn't. But I could hear them pretty clearly, despite the rush of the traffic, because I stood so close.

They talked about what was going on. The actual funeral had been at a church up the road. Just family. This was for everybody else. A kid had died. He'd killed himself. I listened very closely as they talked, and one of them said he'd ridden his skateboard under a bus, on purpose. People had seen him do it. It was some kid I probably didn't know. Some prep school kid Laura must have known; she knows lots of kids.

Hell. I can think of a lot of ways to die, but that's the last way I'd choose.

The people started coming out, carrying flowers to their cars. They were all leaving. I was going to leave too. But the men had mentioned where the burial was going to be. I knew the place, and it wasn't too far.

I didn't really want to go. I mean, this was private, and I'd seen those women in there crying, really crying.

But I had to see her again. Just once more.

So when the bus came I got on it and rode a few miles.

I got off in this neighborhood near downtown, a sort of rough area full of dirty row houses. Rough neighborhoods don't bother me. You walk with your face down, but you always look everywhere. You cross the street if anybody up ahead looks at all threatening. So as not to get stranded, you stay out of alleys and never cross a bridge alone on foot—you find another way around. It's really no problem for me.

I walked until I got to this stone wall, and I went up some stairs. I saw the cars parked in a long line on a gravel road winding through the grass. I saw Laura's car. They were already there.

I stood back for a while, watching. The graveyard was huge, that old famous one on Greenmount Avenue; it's got this big stone church with a really high black steeple. The trees were thick in places, and very green. The grass was very green too. Everything was really quiet and still; all I heard was the traffic away in the street and crows cawing.

I walked from tree to tree. The tombstones slid past me, the old marble like dirty chalk, the names and dates filled with soot. I didn't read them. I watched the burial, coming closer and closer to it.

I came up behind the crowd. They all wore pretty fancy clothes. But then again there were guys like Jack in just jeans and a button-down. I was dressed okay. Nobody noticed me. I didn't bump anybody.

I slid ahead until I was standing two feet behind Laura. I knew it was her, even though she was wearing a veil. I thought only married women were supposed to do that. I mean widows. But she wore one. Her shoulders were beautiful, bare under the straps of her dress and below the veil. I smelled the freshness of her hair. She was sobbing horribly, and shaking.

Her mom and Jack and a few other people were standing around her. Her mom didn't seem to know what to do; if anything, she looked embarrassed, her face sort of stricken, and her eyes, too. I could see that from the side of her face as she nervously looked around. But Jack at least patted Laura's back.

I wanted to touch her.

I wanted to reach out and put my hand on her arm and tell her I was there.

But I didn't.

What good would it have done?

She didn't love me anymore, she'd told me. Nothing I did would make her feel any better.

I started walking backwards, slowly. I'd seen her. That was enough. I didn't know why she was crying. Maybe it was a boy I didn't know about. She'd never told me much about her other friends. Maybe she loved him. I didn't mind. He was dead. I felt bad for her.

I walked backwards until I was out of the crowd. Somebody was saying a few words, but I didn't listen—it was just a man's voice, sharp in the stillness.

They were lowering the coffin into the grave when I turned and walked out of the cemetery.

Nobody had seen me. They'd have needed a picture to know I was there.

Now, that's hiding. Real hiding.

CHAPTER

TWO

I can't tell you what this is all about.

I mean what started with the thing with my elbow.

I mean not yet.

Really, what I want to do here, if you haven't already guessed, is tell you about my *all-time greatest job of hiding,* but I can't just come right out and say where I was when I hid or exactly why I was hiding.

First, it has to do with a lot of things—I mean there were a number of different *reasons* why I hid—and if I just jump ahead and tell you all about it, and especially about what finally happened, you'll think I'm really weird or I'm just making it all up.

Well, maybe I am a *little* weird.

But I'm not making anything up, so please don't start

thinking that. Not because my story is in any way unbelievable, but even I'll agree that things like what I'm about to say just don't happen to people like me.

You see, I'm one of those unique people to whom nothing really big ever happened.

I'm not feeling sorry for myself. Please don't think that, either. But it's just true that nothing big ever happened to me. I've never won a trophy or a prize or anything, or even had my number come up in a raffle. I've never even been on a real vacation; we could never afford it. I know kids who ski and scuba dive and go all over the place; my neighborhood is full of them. But I haven't.

Maybe one day I will. I was talking to a girl I know and I said I think my life will start when maybe I'm twenty-five. She thought that was depressing, but not me. I hoped it would. I mean, I hated thinking I might have to wait until I was *thirty-five*.

What I can tell you right now is what was happening when it all started, but even for that you need to go back a few months, when I think about it.

Three months ago the big event in my life was that Laura dumped me. I can honestly say it was the biggest event that had ever happened to me in my whole life. She was my first girlfriend, and I'm sixteen, so you know how that is.

If you don't, I'll tell you.

I worshiped her.

That's what wrecked everything.

You see, I have some perspective on it now. I can see things a lot clearer. At the time—I mean when we were actually going out, which we really hardly ever did, I mean on real dates; we mainly just met up a bunch of times at my house or a park or the house where she baby-sat—I couldn't see anything clearly at all.

All I could see was her.

I never wanted to see anything else.

I *couldn't* see anything else.

That was the bliss of it. I felt so good being with her that everything else just sort of went away. That's why I think I worshiped her. I mean, that all adds up to worship.

But you can't worship a girl. It's just not fair. It can even be boring.

Boring for her, I mean.

Now, in case you're wondering how I ever got so philosophical and intelligent about all this, don't worry—it's not me. I didn't think of any of that. It all came from my mother. When I was with Laura I spent a lot of time talking about her with my mom. I sure as hell couldn't talk about her with my dad. Even after we broke up, he just didn't care, because this was right about the time he started moping around so much, for reasons I'll get to in a second.

My mom was interested that I finally had a girlfriend, and wanted to tell me things so I wouldn't mess it up, because when she asked me how I felt about Laura and I told her, to tell the truth, she looked a little worried.

And she would know. My mom did a lot of dating in her day when she was a teen—and I guess she was pretty good at it because she wound up marrying my dad when she was nineteen. Maybe she was *too* good at it, because when I think about it, nineteen's still pretty young.

She wouldn't really *talk* but just sort of recited from her roster of thoughts about how it is with boys and girls and love and everything, and I will admit that I did get a lot out of what she said. But I didn't actually accept it all as a sort of, like, *gospel* of truth, because in lots of ways—though she never actually *admitted* it—what she told me about how to treat girls was sort of like a criticism of how my dad was. I mean, if she said a boy should do some particular thing, or *not* do it, it was usually in *reaction* to something I knew for a *fact* had to do with my dad.

Anyways, it was her who told me that you can't worship a girl. They don't like it. She said if you get too gushy, they start to feel sort of embarrassed by it, and even *ignored* after a while, like you're in love with love and not really *them,* and they start to wonder, you know, if it's *real.*

That kind of surprised me.

What's funny is that my mom left my dad just a few days after Laura left me. That's the reason why my dad got totally bummed out, but to tell the truth, things hadn't been so hot between them for months.

He tried keeping it together, but after she left, he stopped going to work. I mean, it's not like he can't go *back* or anything, because he sells real estate and works for himself and can take as much time off as he wants, but he just sort of lost all his vital energy, which is what he always said.

I can't really say what happened between them. I mean, my mom always complained about how there was never enough money, which is what made my dad mope around a lot, because he felt it was a problem he just didn't know how to solve.

But other than that they loved each other a lot. My dad was really kind of crazy about my mom. They were crazy about each other. A kid can tell.

Then something happened, and everything changed.

They never really told me about it. It was obviously something personal—something very, very personal that you just can't explain to your kid. And after my mom left, my dad just lay around on the couch, mainly, watching TV.

Anyways, the night this all started was like that. He was on the couch. The TV was on. I was standing in the hall and I could see him. He looked sort of dazed, or glazed, really—I mean his eyes looked glazed, shining in the dark with little moving pictures of the idiotic show he was watching. I swear he seemed hypnotized.

Now, usually under these sort of circumstances when he sees me out there, he'll look over and ask me something, usually whether I want to play rummy, because he's a big rummy fan and used to play it with my mom all the time.

But this night I'm talking about, which was right at the end of last August—right at the end of summer vacation—he didn't say anything. He just lay there like a zombie, wearing the same old T-shirt he'd had on since that morning when he'd gone out to clip the hedges.

To tell the truth, I knew exactly how he felt. After Laura left me—after she'd told me how her mom had said I was "just a boy" and that she didn't see me as a guy who'd grow up to "accomplish anything important" like Laura's dad and everything—I used to mope around a lot too. I'd also lie in bed watching TV shows, stuff I'd never even heard of. I felt so wiped out, I mean so incredibly *devastated* that Laura had insisted we had to break up, that I just couldn't move, and I was tired all the time, I mean so *completely* and *totally* exhausted, that all I could do was lie around, which of course just intensified how much I was thinking about her.

All I could think about was how beautiful she'd become when she'd left me.

I mean, she was beautiful when we met, but the funny thing was that she became more and *more* beautiful, until she really did become, at least for me, truly the most beautiful girl in the world, which finally happened the day she said we had to break up.

You wouldn't believe how she told me, either.

She said, "My mom says you're just a boy."

We were standing on this playground behind my old elementary school. We used to go there a lot just for privacy, but this time there were lots of kids on the jungle gym and I heard their voices and saw them running around.

I instantly knew what Laura's words implied, and it made me feel terrible, like I was stuck being just like the little kids on the jungle gym and I'd never really grow up.

I looked at her darkly, and said, "What else should I be? I *am* a boy. Does she want you to go out with somebody older? Does she want you to go out with a *man?*"

"That's a pretty stupid thing to say," she said, like I was mocking her mom's wisdom. She winced at me. "Don't be so sarcastic!"

"I can't help it," I said. "I *feel* sarcastic." I felt my voice tremble. "Are you leaving me?"

"*Yes,*" she said.

I just looked at her. Her face was so incredibly beautiful —so hard and cold and incredibly beautiful. And the awful thing was that it was becoming more and *more* beautiful every second, like it was somehow becoming *exponentially* more beautiful, to use a math phrase, because isn't that how things get with a girl when she's ending everything and you just can't stop it? And her eyes, which are dark brown, by the way, sort of very liquid dark brown, looked so incredibly hard. I knew her mind was made up about us no longer being together, and nothing I could say would ever make a difference, and I just couldn't stand it.

"I've thought about it a lot," she said, watching the kids play, so all I could see was the side of her face. Then she turned to me, her beautiful face hard as stone. "I agree with my mom. She can't understand why we're together. She says you're doing nothing with your life. You're just not an achiever. She said that. I agree with her. You'll never accomplish anything important. She's right."

I couldn't believe what I was hearing. I mean, I didn't want to put her mom down, but really, how did she know what I would be when I'm older?

Maybe I *will* accomplish something important.

I probably won't, that's true—I mean, there's certainly no *groundwork* for that ever happening, and certainly my dad didn't do much to kind of *propel* me ever going in that direction, so maybe she was totally right, but it just sounded so mean and petty.

Not that the idea hadn't already sort of occurred to me.

Like, sure, of course it had, and I'd even seen that book called *Rich Dad Poor Dad,* all about how only successful dads can raise successful kids, and I must admit the whole *theme* of it completely bummed me out, because who can really go laying these sort of *curses* on a kid?

What Laura said hurt so bad I could hardly talk. But what I did manage to say was I thought her mom couldn't say that for sure about me, because nobody knows what will happen to them later on, and that anyways I thought my life would begin when I was twenty-five.

I know I already told you I said that, but I think it's important for you to know that it was Laura I was talking to, and she got a little depressed by it, like I said.

At first I thought it was a very clever, relationship-saving thing to say, because it did, at least, suggest that maybe in the *future* I might have a sort of turnaround. I even wanted to tell her how I'd made *plans* all about it, *hidden* plans that I'd never told anybody, about how when I was twenty-five I'd be old enough to be on my own and get out of my nosy neighborhood and live downtown in some big old empty hotel, and that she could even do it *with* me, and we'd be free to kind of be *anonymous* and just be *ourselves* away from anyone who wanted to tell us what to do or be or anything like that. For months I'd really *dreamed* and *hoped* about that and made all *kinds* of plans, especially since I'd met her.

But the truth is, saying the thing about being twenty-five only worked totally against me and buried me even deeper, because she was obviously looking for further reasons to dump me—I could see that she needed them—because her eyes looked hard, like I said, but still had a little sympathy—I could detect just the *dimmest* little glint of sympathy—but that little glint extinguished completely, and she said, "I can't wait that long. I need a boy whose life begins right now. I just can't love you anymore."

And that was that. That ended it. She walked off. I saw she was crying really hard, but she didn't turn when I called after her, so what difference did tears make?

What I didn't understand was a look I saw in her face right before she walked off. It was like maybe she loved me but she wouldn't give in to it, and it, like, *tortured* her. I'd never seen anything so terrible, and I swear I didn't just *imagine* it. I mean, I could *see* her face sort of *trembling* with a struggle, because right under the coldness I saw such warmth and beauty and sadness and humanity, which is what I *always* saw in her face, and I think it was meant for *me*.

But it didn't matter. Her mind was made up. I didn't say a thing. I just watched her walk away, crying.

I can't even tell you how my stomach felt. I was losing

her forever, and it reminded me of building some incredibly intricate thing, like some big complicated Tinkertoy thing I might have made as a kid, and now it was all falling apart and all I wanted to do was locate the secret crux place where I could reconnect things so it would stay standing, and I'm fumbling around everywhere but I can't find the secret *crux* place, because no matter where I reach and grab and try to steady it, the thing just keeps falling until it goes *ka-plotch*.

Anyways, that's why I knew how my dad felt. I sort of related to it. And probably his ka-plotch was even worse than mine—I mean, it *had* to be, because after all, I wasn't *married* to Laura or anything. We hadn't even *talked* about marriage, although I will admit that the idea had certainly occurred to me many times.

But with my dad, he'd been married to my mom for, like, seventeen years and they'd had *me*, for god sakes, so I knew he was having a very hard time, and I will say that I felt pretty sorry for him, although in all honestly he was not too much fun to hang out with—I mean, it had gotten to the point where I could barely stand seeing him just lying around, and all I could think of at that moment was going outside to sort of get away from him.

So I said, "Hey, Dad. I'm going to go take a walk for a while."

He didn't even answer me—just sort of made a little groan and maybe waved his hand.

I waved back, and in a few seconds I was out the door and crossing the yard in the dark.

CHAPTER
THREE

The porch light was out in front of our house because my dad had forgotten to turn it on, and as I came across the grass I saw all these hedge clippings lying all over the place, because he'd sort of given up doing the clipping when he was only halfway done and didn't bag everything up and take it out back like he usually does. I guess he just didn't have the energy; that whole summer he'd complained about never having much *vital* energy. For a second I thought I'd bag the clippings, because the lawn did look a little shabby, and in my neighborhood, certain nosy neighbors —*especially* our next-door neighbor—are very sensitive about things like that. But to tell the truth, I felt sort of tired already because it was pretty late, and I knew there'd be no harm in waiting to bag it all up in the morning.

I left my yard and crossed the street beside my house and went over to where this big red-brick building is, and I crept into the shadows behind some hedges and stood still. You see, in my neighborhood, just like I mentioned with my next-door neighbor, you have to be careful, because people, in a way, are always sort of *spying* on you.

My next-door neighbor—his name is Mr. Miller, by the way, and he used to be the dean of this girls' college out in Harford County, but he's retired now—actually sits on his porch every day—you can see him through the gray screens —and I swear if he's not *watching* for the slightest disunity in the houses and yards all around him—and especially in *our* house, because it's closest—then I don't know what he's doing out there. At least this is what my dad has always said about him, and I have to say I agree.

People in my neighborhood really are a bit nosy—actually more than a bit. I think it's why they move here, if only to exercise that option. My dad says that too, and he's lived here all his life, so he ought to know. He says you have to watch out because what the neighbors do is start casting *aspersions* on you if you aren't careful to do everything right. They keep up on you. I don't mean like a Neighborhood Watch to look out for vagrants and outsiders or things getting stolen or kids coming up on porches and wrecking stuff—although there has been plenty of that around where I live, and I even know lots of kids who have done it. I don't mean that sort of criminal stuff, because about that, naturally, all anybody'd do is call the cops and have the person arrested, and he'd be in trouble and have to pay the penalty, et cetera, et cetera.

It's a different kind of thing I'm talking about.

A *different* kind of trouble.

In my neighborhood it's like you feel you're in trouble *all* the time, but you know you haven't really done anything to deserve it. So you keep trying to do *little* things to get yourself out of the trouble you feel you don't even deserve, little things like keeping your yard perfectly straight or your house perfectly painted and your car new or at least perfectly clean. Because if you don't, you feel you'll have to pay some sort of awful penalty, although in the absolute truth, nobody ever says what the penalty might be, or even what the rules are that you're trying to keep up with. It's really kind of an easy place to sort of look *down* on yourself all the time, because you get to feel everybody has maybe a sort of snooty *attitude* toward you and your whole family, and when you come right down to it, they don't think you really *belong*. And I don't mean just little things like bagging up your clippings right away after cutting them, but more important stuff like what people think of the school you go to or what your dad does for a living.

It's a place where people can sort of act like you don't even *exist*, even if they actually know you really well and used to be your friends, which is exactly what happened with Mr. Miller's niece and nephew, who are twins my age. We used to play together all the time when they came by to spend the day with their uncle. But one day I came out when they were chucking this ball to each other in their yard, and they didn't come into mine when I asked them. They didn't even *look* at me. Then one of them, *still* without looking at me, said, "We're not allowed to play with you anymore."

I stood there speechless for a minute.

Then I asked, *"Why?"*

But neither of them answered. They just went on chucking the ball back and forth like a couple of zombies. It occurred to me to maybe yell at them or go in their yard to get their attention, but from the blank zombie looks on their faces, I just didn't *want* to. I mean, it didn't really seem to be *worth* it, and anyways, I figured it would probably just make things worse. So I just stood there looking at them, feeling kind of sick, until I went back in my house.

I don't know what it was. I never found out. Maybe Mr. Miller had heard my parents arguing too loud or maybe he thought something was wrong with our house. It's impossible to say, but from that day on, those kids acted like I wasn't even there.

And let me tell you, it's experiences like *that*—and I've had *plenty* of them—that put your imagination in a certain place, a certain sort of paranoid place, so it's really no wonder why I went around hiding all the time.

Maybe this all sounds crazy to you and you've never heard of a neighborhood like mine. But I've been around a bit and seen lots of other neighborhoods, and I know for a fact that my neighborhood's not the only one like that, believe me.

So when I crossed the street this night I am telling you about, I made sure to leave my yard at the farthest possible point from the streetlight on the corner, and I dashed across the street like a shadow, because you never know when somebody might be watching.

True, I didn't see anybody at any window, and you better believe I'd paused to take a look. I didn't even see any *light* at any window, so I realized it was probably a little later than I'd thought, probably almost midnight, maybe even later, because now, when I considered it, my dad had been watching one of those long sales shows on TV, one of those celebrity-hosted infomercial sales shows—I think it was about a new kind of blender—and usually they only sell cable time for that sort of junk way past prime time.

But nobody was watching me, at least as far as I could tell.

Still, it actually looked like the *houses* were watching, because they all had this sort of dark, shuttered look, and they all look a little similar anyway, all built on variations of the same sort of plan just like my house, with three stories and slanted roofs and brown shingles, and windows on the second level that look like lidded eyes if you factor in the shades, and porches with low roofs and fence railings that with only the barest added imagination always look like a grinning mouth with gritted teeth.

Anyways, I just stood there.

Hidden.

In the bushes.

Or rather, behind this long hedge that runs along the bottom of this concrete ramp that leads up to the entrance doors of this big red-brick building, which by the way is the only commercial building for miles around, because my neighborhood really isn't zoned for business.

The air felt pretty cool. I hadn't brought my windbreaker. That was a big bummer, because I own a pretty good windbreaker; my mom had bought it for me just about a week before she left. But I didn't have it on me, and I sure wasn't going to go back into the house to get it.

Suddenly, it occurred to me that it was a pretty dumb idea to take a walk. It was late and it was getting cold. I mean, it was probably only sixty-five degrees outside, but compared to the heat of the day that was bad enough.

I wrapped my arms around myself—I suddenly felt so cold and it seemed so late. True, tomorrow wasn't a school day or anything. Some of the local schools had already started, especially the private ones—during the day I'd seen kids in uniforms walking home. I was still on vacation, but it was pretty late to just be roaming around.

Through the hedge I could see the street. I tried to

consider my options. I could go down through the woods to the farm store; it was still open. My house is on a hill—at the bottom there's this strip of woods with a stream, and beyond that the street rises up another pretty steep hill crowded with more houses. If I went to the farm store I could go through the woods, which would be spooky as hell, but at least I wouldn't be seen by anybody. My friend Carol and I had done that a few times, on these nights when we'd sneak out together just for fun. The woods are maybe a mile long and there's this open-all-night farm store I mentioned pretty much right at the end of them.

But I'd never gone through the woods alone, and to tell you the truth, it sort of spooked me, because there's the usual empty wooden sheds and stuff along the trail, and even this old abandoned church graveyard that totally freaks me out, and freaked out Carol even more, because he used to be a Catholic school kid and was still very susceptible to those kinds of fears surrounding graveyards and stuff.

But the truth is, I didn't have any money, and anyway, without having Carol around I wouldn't have anybody to talk to, which was really all the fun of why we ever did it in the first place. So that option was out.

Next I thought about how if I went up the hill in the dark, I'd pass through this richer neighborhood called Oaks, or *The* Oaks if you want to get really technical about it. If I passed through there, I'd finally get to this business district about two miles away, with sub shops and gas stations and this whole sort of poor, rundown neighborhood of flimsy houses beyond it called Greenway Terrace, which has an atmosphere I sort of like—don't ask me why—except that I'd been there scads of times to visit my grandma. My grandma still lives there in the same house my mom grew up in, and never sold it, even though my grandpa died, like, almost sixteen years ago, just a few months after I was born.

I spent my whole childhood with my grandma—I mean my mom's mom—and she's like a classic grandma and really pretty nice, with those wire glasses and white hair that's like a cloud because she goes to those beauty parlors, and when I was little she always used to baby-sit me.

She usually came to my house, but sometimes—especially on weekends, because this was back when my parents used to go out pretty late together on sort of dates, and my grandma didn't want to get home too late—I'd spend the night at her house, sleeping in my mom's old room, which still had some of her stuff in it, dolls and pennants and things, from when she was a kid.

My grandma's house is pretty small and sort of cramped, but full of sofas and raggy quilts, so it's super cozy. I'd sit in this crazy recliner chair that went all the way back, and she'd bring out these old lacy photo albums full of pictures of my grandpa before he died, from a long time ago when he was in the army, and she would put them in my lap. She even had some pictures of my mom when she was a teen, and Grandma told me there used to be lots more of them. But my mom had torn up a bunch because she hated how she looked with one of those big hairdos that Greenway Terrace girls had back then, though I thought she looked really pretty.

We always had a great time, Grandma and me, but the big event was that right before it got dark, we'd take a walk down to the street where the shops were, and she'd buy me a Coke or something before we walked home.

I know it sounds silly saying it was a big event, but Greenway Terrace seemed like a whole different world to me. It was like I was on *vacation.* I remember thinking how *different* and simpler it all was from my neighborhood, where life felt like a game of hopscotch you had to play with a blindfold on. I've always been pretty sensitive to how people look at me. But up there in Greenway Terrace I never felt like everybody was sort of *staring* at me and *wondering* what I was all about. I always felt freer in Greenway Terrace, like I could do what I wanted and just be *myself.* I mean, I did sort of feel pretty *anonymous,* but in a really good way. And my grandma without even trying was, like, really *supportive* with all that, because unlike the people down the hill, she never put any pressure on me to be anything other than what I already am. I mean, for some crazy reason she seemed *satisfied* with that.

Anyways, I thought about how we always had a great time together, my grandma and me. I thought I should probably go visit her again soon, to let her know she still had a grandson.

I didn't have to worry about visiting my dad's parents, though. They moved away right after I was born and let my dad have their house, which, funny enough, is the same one *he* grew up in.

I sort of got the idea that my dad never really liked his parents too much, but I must admit he never actually talked about it. He would talk a lot about *some* things, especially the neighborhood, because he really did like *dissecting* the neighborhood into what he called all its *levels,* which is something he sort of *infected* me with, because I know I do that a lot too. But other things he never talked about and never tried to figure out—I mean like his parents. Of course, nobody ever tries to figure out that sort of stuff too much anyways, so I can't really blame him.

But it was never like that with my mom's mom. We always got along great.

So I decided to go to Greenway Terrace.

Well, I won't say that I exactly *decided* to go there, but that was the direction in which I headed, just sort of ambling along without a plan, and running between the streetlights to get warmer after I'd scoped out the house windows to make sure no one was watching and checked the street for cars.

Now, I know you're going to think I'm lying right now.

I mean about my intentions.

You're definitely going to think I'm lying, especially after I told you about me going to the funeral, because I'm sure you've realized that I walked exactly the same way that day.

But before I say anything more about what I did, all I can really say is, I didn't *have* any intentions at all.

None whatsoever.

Like I already said, I was going up the hill past all the watching houses to go through The Oaks to get to Greenway Terrace, which was a dumb name for the place, because I don't think a single house on any street up there actually had a terrace, and if it did, it was probably littered with junk like old washing machines and spare tires.

I was just going up the street, and I finally got to the big intersection that's a four-way and all lit up, and there was nothing I could do to not get seen except just wait for the light to change, which I did, and I was lucky no cars came by and nobody saw me.

I got over into The Oaks, and I've got to say that I liked it there—I always have. For one thing, it smells really good. When they picked the name *The Oaks* they weren't kidding, because in the air there's this very verdant sort of smell, like in a forest, heavy and green, because the trees up there are so thick that's where you think you are. And unlike my neighborhood down the hill, most of the houses in The Oaks—which by the way are these really big houses made of stones, almost like castles in France—they don't stare, but just sort of *peek* out behind these big trees and bushes, and all you can see are the edges of them, even though they are so damned huge.

I knew I'd be in trouble if I got spotted here — because believe me, these people up in The Oaks are sort of extra special cautious about looking after their property — so I started going through yards, behind bushes. I went through yards on Whitley Avenue and then cut over through a back alley to White Oak Lane, and then when some dog started barking behind a fence I cut back to Whitley.

I started walking slower.

I looked over, and saw a certain house.

And I stopped.

It was Laura's house.

CHAPTER

FOUR

All right. You think I'm lying.

Well, maybe I am.

It's true I thought about her all the time. I mean, like I said, even seeing my dad lying on the couch made me think of her, because of the similarities, you know, between my situation and his, which I certainly did relate to, and was one of the reasons, and probably the big *main* reason, I'd gone out in the first place, just to escape that sort of claustrophobic feeling in the house, that mopey feeling my dad always had.

But if I did have any intentions, believe me, they were buried.

They were subliminal.

I mean subconscious.

I really hadn't had any *foresight* in the matter at all. It's just that this was the path I'd always taken to get to her house on the days I'd walked there, the same path I used to walk when we were still together. I mean, I was used to it. So it was probably just some sort of *osmosis* that made me take the same path again, even though it was, of course, the same thing I had done on the day of the funeral.

I wasn't—and you're, of course, probably thinking I was, and you have every right to think it—just some nut kid who sneaked up the street to spy on his ex-girlfriend's house late at night.

But you can go on not believing me. That's okay, because I'm pretty sure you'll change your mind when you hear the whole story.

Of course, I have to admit that once I saw the place, I didn't want to leave.

Now you're probably laughing at me. But that's okay too.

Her house just looked so peaceful. In every home on the street the lights were out—hers too. And I had to get closer to her house. I couldn't just stay in the street. Some weird patrol car might come by. They had that sort of thing up there.

I ducked aside to get a better look and even see that cast-iron furniture we used to sit on some nights when I came over. It was still there, just beyond some smaller trees in her yard—her huge, *huge* yard—all the furniture like a little cast-iron haven, surrounded by bushes and vines tangled through the frame of this nifty domed gazebo.

I came right up under the gazebo and stood there looking at the table and chairs for a minute, all of it painted black and barely visible in the dark. I bet there'd been a sprinkler on in the yard earlier, because I gently ran my hand over the cast-iron table and felt it was beaded with water.

I stepped out and walked across the yard very quietly, dodging from tree to tree. Next to the house was a big swath of bushes, maybe fifteen feet high, and they cast a wide shadow over the grass. I stepped into the shadow. I looked both ways first. Across the front street there was nothing. Just some parked cars shining under a street lamp, and a mailbox on the corner. The houses across the street were just as quiet. Some blue light in a single window, maybe somebody still up watching TV.

A car drove past. I froze. I didn't even duck down.

It was a police car.

I was wearing dark stuff, blue jeans that were new and still very dark blue and stiff, and a black T-shirt with long sleeves. In the shadows I really couldn't've been seen. I knew it. I mean, I felt pretty confident about that. I was standing too still. They say ninjas do that, just as I was doing it. I read about it in a magazine, one of those karate magazines you find in some places, magazine racks in grocery stores. You can also see it in karate movies. They stand very still in the shadows—ninjas, I mean—beside a bush, and unless someone is very observant, they think the ninja is just part of the bushes. He might even angle his arms a little, just to look more like a bush. When I froze I was sort of midstep, and I bet I looked just like a bush.

The cop drove on, slowly. He didn't use his spotlight and shine it over the grass. If he looked in my direction at all, he just saw bushes and didn't notice me.

But I looked hard at him. I was staring at the car—my head was turned that way—and when it got to the intersection about fifty yards up the street I could see the driver through the open window, because the lights at the intersection were all pretty bright.

It wasn't a man at all, but a woman, a woman cop I'd seen around a few times in the neighborhood and up at the grocery, this woman cop with a young-looking face that's kind of round and pretty, but with a blunt nose that makes her look sort of tough.

I kind of knew her. I mean, I'd talked with her once. I'd said hello to her in the line at the grocery a few months ago, but she just nodded at me with this strange sort of smile. I'd said hello because some guys I know, when we get to talking about such things, said that women cops are meaner than men cops, because maybe they have something to prove. But that wasn't true at all with this woman cop. She didn't seem mean at all, just tough, and I wanted to thank her for looking out for the people in the neighborhood. I thought she might like that.

We didn't get a talk going. To tell you the truth, her smile was sort of weird, that kind where she thinks maybe it's all a trick or not sincere or she's being made fun of. I figured she didn't really trust me wanting to talk to her at all, so I just sort of dropped it. But she wasn't mean or anything, at least to me. She had copper-colored hair, the same color as copper wire. Right now, sitting in the car, her hair was up in a bun, and she turned her head a little, and then the light changed and she drove off into the darkness across the intersection between rows of houses on both sides of the street. All I could see were her taillights receding into the dark, until even they went away down the hill and I was totally alone again.

So like a ninja I just waited and listened.

I didn't hear a thing.

The blue light went off in the house across the street.

I smiled at that.

Sometimes in my house my dad falls asleep on the couch with the TV on and it stays on all night. If you try to turn it off he'll wake up and get pretty angry, so I never even try anymore. To turn it off, I mean. But obviously this person was in bed, probably, because the light had been on the second floor, and it went out.

After a minute I thought it was safe to move, so I moved very slowly, dropping down to my knees and crawling into the bushes planted right alongside the house in a trench of black soil. I kind of crawled on my fingertips and shoe tips, keeping my knees off the ground, even though it felt pretty awkward, so as not to get muddy, because the soil was pretty moist, and

I could smell it, heavy and cold and ashy in the wind that was blowing lightly through the yard.

I passed as quietly as possible through the bushes. My back scraped the leaves. They were these hard little conifer leaves like tiny green shells — I think they're called conifers, because I did some gardening once for a lady who had them in her yard, and that's what she called them. Whatever noise I made scraping through them, anybody listening would have thought it was the wind, which was moving the bushes up top where the branches spread out a little, making just the same sort of quiet, rustling noise.

When I was all the way through I stood straight. There was a space about a foot and a half wide between the bushes and the house. I could stand in it, completely hidden. It even blocked the breeze that was blowing. I felt warmer. The truth is, it was getting pretty cold. That happens sometimes here at night, even in August, and it means autumn's coming early.

I stood on a tangle of roots and wiped my fingertips on the stone wall of the house. I didn't want to get the wall dirty, but I had to clean my hands. Anybody looking in my direction would never have seen me. Only the closest observer might have looked down and seen my pants legs — the shadow of them, I mean. But they were so dark, and my sneakers were black. I was totally ninja, blending completely into the bush.

You have to know about the stone wall, though. This house was great.

Laura's house.

It was twice the size of mine, maybe three times. And it was made of a zillion of these big slate stones, held together with concrete. It was totally unlike the houses where I live, just a few blocks down the street—the same street the woman cop had driven down. The houses there are all made of shingles, some in better repair than others, and there's nothing worse than bad shingles to make a house look beat-up; they look like broken teeth. The shingles on my house are okay, I guess. My dad does pretty good upkeep.

But this stone wall was amazing.

I'd always wanted to live in a house made like this. Down where I am it's true that the houses are older. They're *much* older, and some of the people have a sort of attitude about that, like it makes them more a part of the neighborhood, the original part, by which they mean the better part.

I must admit my dad's like that, because he's third genera-tion, and he's pretty proud of that, and in fact when my mom gets on him for not having made much money, he always says that even though that's true, he did get her out of Greenway Terrace, which to him is, like, the biggest deal in the world, but really only serves to piss her off. And she always says he should have moved, because the neighborhood *sapped* his ambition —she always says that, that it really *sapped his ambition*—and he never has much of an answer to that at all, because I think he actually agrees with it.

But up here across the intersection the houses are stone and the people are richer, all of them are richer. I'm sure you know what I mean. But also everything is newer, and people come and go a lot—some families stay only a few years and you never even get to know their names, whereas where I live, just a few blocks away, you can meet people like Mr. Reynolds, whom I've done yard work for, and he's been living in that old dump of his for his whole life. He's sixty or something and wears a wooden leg, and his father lived his whole life there too, and the whole house is crammed floor to ceiling with boxes of junk from both their lifetimes, because Old Man Reynolds—that's what we call him—he's a hoarder. That's my neighborhood. But here people come and go a lot, and renovate a lot, so things always look perfect.

I stood very still, lightly brushing my hand on the stones, when a thought occurred to me.

If I lived in this house, I'd be happier.

I couldn't help thinking that.

Anybody would be happier in this house because it was just so great, so stately and magnificent. I looked up and saw these box windows hovering over me, about ten feet above me.

To just sit in there looking out the window.

You could never feel trapped.

You couldn't *hide* in this house; it wasn't that kind of place.

No—you were really kind of on *display* in this house.

You'd always feel alive inside.

I mean you could *breathe.*

Up here it seemed there were no rules except for the ones you make yourself, but just down the hill you always felt exhausted trying to follow everybody *else's* rules, which they never even bothered to explain to you. My dad calls it the difference between the freedom of luxury and the burden of maintenance. I call it a launch pad instead of a trap.

I bet everybody in there, Laura especially, but probably also her entire family, woke every morning happy to jump out of bed, to go down to the kitchen—the kitchen that I'd never seen but knew must be amazing—to eat breakfast and talk with the family and get ready to go out for the day. And when they were out they'd know the house was always there, waiting. But not waiting in a bad way, in a foreboding way like my house was always waiting, because the people here moved on a lot like I said, to even newer houses in even better places. Yet while they were here their house was bright and clean and new and pleasant, with all these cool new things in it, in the kitchen especially, I bet, all these gewgaws that do everything for you, not like the old crap from the 1950s you see in kitchens down the hill that you get from your great-grandmother. It was a house for people who take trips to the Bahamas, I thought, like Laura had done lots of times with her mom and dad. The first night I met her she told me she'd just come from the Bahamas, and she was smoothing lotion on her peeling nose because she'd gotten too much sun. Probably everybody on her street went there as well; they probably saw one another every summer down on some sunny island in the sea, whereas people just down the hill where I live were always stuck in their houses, or at best out doing something in the yard or piling boxes of old junk in their basement or garage.

I rubbed my hand on the wall, lightly. I wanted to scrape the dirt off my fingers respectfully; I really didn't want to mess up the stones. The truth is, I kept thinking about how *perfect* life must be in this house, and the silly thought came to me that it would be *impossible* to have problems in this house.

I know how that sounds. I mean, of course there would be problems; I'm not naive enough to think everything would just be bliss. So I suppose I meant that in this house I couldn't possibly have *my* problems, the same old problems I'd always had that were never going away, like hearing my parents gripe about money or feeling stuck forever in the same place. Houses like mine were made for people who want to get morose about their problems—witness my dad back there, lying on the couch.

I'd still have problems. Sure.

But *different* problems. I'd probably have a whole *new* set of problems that I'd probably get excited about. And it occurred to me right then that the happiest people must be those who are excited about trying to solve their problems, who see them as challenges, you know, like it says on those posters guidance counselors hang up on the walls of their offices.

But some problems, I'm sure you'll agree, are pretty hard to get excited about.

I'd never been excited about mine even in the least. So of course my problems never went away.

But here—in this house—I thought I'd *like* my problems. I bet I'd even take a crack at solving them.

I mean, seriously, what problems could Laura have?

True—*I* was her problem—but she solved that one quick enough.

I stood silently, gazing up at the shadows of the bushes on the wall. I felt so close to her, closer than I'd been for months.

She was in there.

I knew it.

It's like I could *feel* her presence.

I wondered. If I listened hard enough, might I hear her breathing as she slept?

I shook my head slowly. *Okay. That's getting weird,* I thought.

I took my hand off the wall. I took a deep breath of the cool breeze and grinned, looking down into the dark at my feet.

What's funny was I had never even gone into her house.

Not even once.

She never *took* me in; she always made me wait outside. I

haven't known too many girls—as girlfriends, I mean—but I saw this habit of Laura's as sort of like a trait probably shared by many very special girls. We went out for three months and all I ever saw was just part of the entrance hallway when she'd leave me standing at the front door, because she'd run inside to get something for "just a minute!" but always took, like, at least twenty minutes.

When I think of her house, I mean if I associate any particular house with her, I always think more of where I saw her when she baby-sat, which was just a couple blocks down the street. That house wasn't too much different from her own; I mean at least in terms of its size and how fancy it was.

Laura had let me come into that house plenty of times, but I always had to wait outside awhile. I'd stay in the dark until after the parents left and she'd put the kid to sleep. That usually took at least an hour, and I'd always hide out back—in the alley, actually, where there weren't any lights at all. I'd just sort of hang around waiting, near all the dark garages, and feeling the breeze blowing through the alley, but also feeling this terrific sense of *expectation,* you know, so I never felt bored or lonely. I'd wait until I saw the parents drive out of their garage—I'd hide there in the dark—and after they were gone I'd sneak into their yard.

Of course, Laura really would take an extra long time to let me in, not because she was ignoring me—I mean, I knew she was just as crazy to make out as I was, and she'd even send me these sexy little texts to keep me from dropping dead out there—but the truth is, she totally loved this little kid she baby-sat for. His name was Joey and she talked about him all the time and told me how wonderful he was—like even when he peed his pants it was the most charming thing in the world. I must say she was sort of a sucker for always reading him one more bedtime story, which of course meant, like, *five* more, and giving him snacks and whatever else he wanted to eat, and sometimes I would sneak up and watch through the window as she played clappy games and stuff with him, and I swear it was like she was Joey's frickin' mom or something, though to tell the truth, I had never seen a *real* mom love a kid that much. Maybe a few moms, but not too many, and because I had nothing to do but wait I would even sort of *fantasize* that Laura and me were actually *married* and she'd, like, given *birth* to our son, who of course was supposed to be Joey, and that would keep me sort of occupied while I waited at the window, until she actually put him to sleep and shut out the lights in the house.

Then my phone would buzz and she would whisper, "Come in now. Meet me around back."

She loved inviting me there because she loved secrets; she told me she loved knowing that nobody would ever find us out.

When I came up to the back steps, she'd be standing there with a big smile on her face. The lights would be off.

She'd take my hand and pull me inside. We'd stand there in the living room and start making out. I'd kiss her like I was glued to her, smelling the crazy good perfume she wore. It was incredible.

And then I'd start.

I'd start telling her how wonderful she was.

I must have told her ten thousand times.

"You're wonderful and beautiful; you're wonderful and beautiful. . . ."

I hope sometimes I was just *thinking* it and not saying it, because I know how tiresome it can get hearing the same compliment over and over. That's another thing my mom had told me. She said it might be good if I came up with something fresh once in a while, because you know, always saying the same thing kind of wears it out.

But I couldn't help it. It was true. And even now, standing under the windows, I still said it.

You're wonderful and beautiful.

Some of my friends — well, my friend Carol, who I'll tell you more about later on — had asked me what I saw in her.

"Everything," I told him.

He looked surprised.

So did my mother, when I told her.

But my mother actually understood; she wasn't reacting like my friend, who maybe saw some flaw in Laura I couldn't see or just didn't like her because, you know, she was always pretty quiet and serious, and that could make her seem sort of superior.

Not that he ever really said what the flaw was, because of course I asked him. He agreed she was pretty, but he said he knew how to *read* people — he was always bragging about this intense ability he had to *read* people — and he said it was her *personality* that had the flaw, not her face or anything, but he could *see* it in her face every time he looked at her.

The flaw, I mean.

I swear, I didn't know what he was talking about.

I'll agree she had a withering look. She really did have, sometimes, what people call a withering look. Once she shot a look like that at Carol, and he said to me afterward, "Whoa, man! Does she think I'm *nothing?*"

My mother never even *met* Laura, I mean except maybe once in a hallway for, like, ten minutes, because my mom was rarely around my house. Things were already pretty bad with my dad, and on a couple of occasions, after big fights, she'd leave for a few days to stay at her mom's, my grandma's. I talked the most to my mom during those times — I'd go over there, and talking about Laura kind of got her mind off things with my dad.

I did have a picture of Laura, and my mom agreed she was beautiful. Very beautiful. You see, my mom has an open mind about beauty and isn't hung up on stupid garbage like my idiot friend, who was probably just jealous anyways.

My mother told me a million things.

It was late now. I didn't know how late. It had that after-midnight feel, though, with no cars coming by. It was even cooler, too, almost cold. The soil felt damp under my feet, and then I realized my feet were wet.

I tried moving, very slowly.

Then I stopped.

My feet were tangled in a garden hose.

They had a gardener, I bet; I remembered Laura mentioning something about having one. And he'd left his hose right down there in the soil at my feet, and he must have done plenty of watering in the afternoon, because by now my shoes were completely soaked.

I was getting pretty cold. The last thing I needed was to get sick, too. It would be a nightmare to be stuck in the house with my dad when I was sick.

I bent down, pretty slowly, and in a few seconds I was unraveling this immense hose, which I'd noticed when I stepped on it but had thought it was those roots I mentioned. Except the more I tried to unravel it, the more I succeeded in only sort of tying up my feet; I mean tying them together even worse.

Finally I had to bend down really low — and that's when it happened.

This thing I've been waiting to tell you.

The thing with my elbow.

My elbow tapped the window at the bottom of the stone wall—I mean this sort of narrow transom window that's maybe actually called a hopper window, now that I think about it.

It was open. I could see that the hose at my feet disappeared into the window.

When my elbow hit it—tapped it, I mean, and very gently—it swung back and forth like the hinge was oiled. It sort of really flopped back and forth, and I couldn't help thinking what a great hinge it was, and not like the ones at my house that sound all haunted and creaky, or just let out a rip when you yank them shut—I mean a huge ripping horn sound like an elephant fart.

But this hinge was perfect and silent.

For a while, I just looked at the open window.

My first thought was that I should go home.

But I didn't want to go home.

My dad would still be up.

Not waiting for me.

Just lying there.

Maybe wanting to talk.

I didn't want to talk. I'd had enough of that, believe me.

Maybe, I thought, he'd be asleep with the TV on. You know why I thought that. I already brought it up before. But I doubted it. He was feeling too stressed to sleep. He'd be brooding, waiting to talk.

My feet were, like, glued in the soil. In the muck, really, because the gardener or whoever must have forgotten to close the faucet wherever it was, and the thinnest little trickle was coming out of the end of the hose, which was one of those new hoses that stretches really long and contracts really tight, which is exactly what it had done around my feet. But I managed to get it off, and the sill of the window was just high enough for me to sit on.

So I sat.

And I thought, *Why not go inside?*

It was just a simple thought at first, and as soon as I had it, I got scared. Really petrified. I'd tapped the window and it swung on some sort of spring-loaded or oiled hinge, and I knew it was only a matter of seconds now before an alarm would go off. I'd probably get stuck in the bushes and it would be just a few more seconds before the whole house would be awake and that woman cop would come cruising back with her siren on.

I was really feeling very nervous.

But then I realized that the window was already open.

I mean unlocked.

If there was an alarm—and I remembered Laura telling me how there was, and it was hooked up to this roving squad of vans you see driving all over the neighborhood day and night—it was not connected to this window. Or it was just turned off.

So why not go inside? I thought.

I wasn't going to *do* anything.

I just wanted to get warm.

I'd never seen inside Laura's house, anyways.

Why not take a look?

It was probably a club basement. There was one at the house where she baby-sat; we'd made out down there lots of times on the sofas. A huge club basement full of games and stuff. It'd be the same here, I thought. It'd be neat to just take a quick look.

A quick look, and then go.

I took off my shoes and, using the coils of the hose, scraped the mud off them as best I could. I swiveled around, which was tough to manage on that narrow sill, but I'm pretty skinny.

I went in face first. I was so quiet, the breeze made more noise than me.

I was halfway inside when I realized it was a straight drop in the pitch dark. I could scale down, though, because the wall was covered with jutting stones that felt sandy and gave me plenty of handholds. And there was a big metal sink right under the window, which gave me more to hang on to and balance myself.

I made my way down, turned myself around, dropped my feet until they touched something solid, and stood.

I was standing in front of the sink, one of those big sturdy ones like metal boxes you see in basements sometimes. I could already tell just by the smell in the air that this was no club basement, but a storage basement; it had that dead grass and gasoline smell.

I reached up, got my shoes, and reached farther to close the window.

But then I did something I can't explain.

I didn't close the window.

I knelt up on the sink, put my hands out the window, and patted down the soil where I'd been standing, so no one would ever know I'd been there. And when I was done with that I cleaned my hands and my shoes with the thinnest trickle of water from the faucet in the sink and wiped them with an already dirty rag that was sitting there, which I could barely see, except by the dim rays of light coming down through the window from the street lamps outside.

When everything seemed clean enough, I stepped off into the dark, holding my shoes in my hands.

FIVE

Now, I know you think I'm crazy.

Maybe like a sicko.

Up to now I don't really know what you thought about me. I suspect you thought I was just some sort of lame, ordinary kid, and I won't argue with you there, because my whole life, to tell you the truth, hasn't given me much to work with to keep me from seeming lame and ordinary. I don't mean *I* think I'm lame and ordinary, but the point is, I can see how people around me do—I mean people in the neighborhood—because I just go to public school and I don't, like, have a car or even know how to drive because my school doesn't offer Driver's Ed, and I must admit I never did sports much or won, like, debates or anything. So I can actually understand why other people might think that about me, and I know lots of them do, but really it's just because they don't take any interest in me because I can't show them a car or trophies or prizes or scholarships, and they never tried to get to know me at all.

But now I go and sneak into my ex-girlfriend's house, and I realize that based on what I've already told you about myself, and because of the opinions you've probably already formed about me—which by the way I don't blame you for, because like I said, I'd probably be the first person to understand your opinions about me, even if they just boiled down to my being lame and ordinary—I think you must be thinking, *Why the hell did you go into her house?*

Are you weird? Are you a stalker?

I stood in the dark asking myself just those same questions, because to tell you the truth, I'd sort of confused myself by doing it—I mean by actually having the *nerve* to go in. I mean, I'd never done anything like it before, not even *remotely* like it. I'd never spied on anybody or followed anybody around, or crank-called anybody, even.

What I told you I had done a lot of was *hiding,* and that's actually the opposite of being a stalker, if you get what I mean. I mean, a stalker is really trying to *pursue* people, but a hider wants to stay as far away from them as possible.

So I want you to know that I think it was wrong to go in. Really wrong.

I mean, I'm actually actively *against* such sorts of behavior, because they remind me of this nut I know named Paul

Stewart, this real psycho nut who I used to talk to sometimes after lunch. He had this huge thing for this girl named Bethany Cooper or Cowper or something like that, and he went around taking pictures of her while she wasn't looking. I mean really sneaky pictures, and I know he actually did it, because he showed me the pictures to prove it, even pictures he took of her when he followed her to the beach, like, a hundred and fifty miles away just for the purpose of spying and came away with these very sexy pictures of her wearing this filmy thing over her bikini like some *Sports Illustrated* model. And even though she was not my type, because I don't actually go for tall blondes and prefer shorter beautiful brown-haired girls like Laura, I will say this Bethany girl was incredibly beautiful in that sort of very popular *Sports Illustrated* way.

But this nut Paul didn't stop there. After he went and took all those pictures and did things with them on the Internet that I don't even want to talk about, because I can't have some weirdo reading this get any vile ideas, he finally got the nerve to get her phone number from some goofy friend of hers, some careless, goofy friend, and one night he starts texting her, and she must have thought he was charming, because they got a little talk going. She was in her house upstairs on the second floor evidently walking around her room or watching TV in her undies up there, and when she finally asked where he was, he said, "I'm out on your roof! Will you let me in?"

He was right outside her frickin' window!

It made the papers, that did, and Bethany was so freaked she got her mom to put out a restraining order on psycho Paul, which just for the record I'll say I totally see the purpose and necessity of, and I'll add that I no longer wanted to talk to him after lunch or anytime else, and I mean ever, because it is not my habit to associate with loony psychos.

But here I go and find Laura's window open, her basement transom hopper window, at what must have been at least midnight and was probably more like one o'clock in the morning, and without even *thinking* about it and giving it any clear thought at all I just climb right in, like it's something I'm really good at and maybe do every day.

I'm telling you, I didn't know what to make of myself.

And the weird thing is, once I was in there and standing in the dark, I didn't know why I'd come in.

The even weirder thing was that I felt there was a *reason*.

I just couldn't tell what it was.

Of course I wanted to get back together with Laura. I'm sure you've already guessed that. But I didn't see how sneaking into her house would help. If anything, I knew it would just destroy whatever chance I might ever possibly have with her, because if she found me in her basement, she'd probably despise me and never speak to me again for her whole life.

My best bet was just to climb back out the window.

But this feeling I had, this feeling of a *reason*, it was really strong.

What worried me was that I really couldn't tell if it was a *good* reason, or whether I was just a nut like Paul Stewart and was obsessed with seeing Laura, or spying on her and trying to catch a glimpse of her sitting around in her undies watching TV, even though while we were together making out where she baby-sat I'd already seen her in her undies, or close to it, so it wasn't like I had some special perverted need to see her like that again.

I mean, even though I'd thought already about how she was asleep up in her room—because I swear I could sort of really *feel* her there, like I could almost hear her *breathing*— I wasn't planning to, like, wait for when everybody else was asleep and go peek in on her. True, she had told me that she slept wearing hardly anything; we were talking one day about it, and I forget how the subject came up—I think it was when she saw these pajamas I wear—and she mentioned that she always slept with no shirt on because she felt comfortable that way, but also I could sort of tell she wanted to impress me with how sexy and mature she was. And I must admit I *did* think about that—I mean I thought about her asleep up there with maybe no shirt on—and I have to admit that I thought that was pretty exciting and might be sort of nice to see—actually *very* nice to see—because Laura is really, really beautiful, like I said, but I mean only if she *wanted* me to see her that way, and not like I wanted to just go and *peek* in on her like some total weirdo.

I thought being down there was wrong.

I really did.

I felt really nervous and even had this weird sense of dizzines—from so much excitement I guess—and thought the best thing to do was just climb right back out of there.

But the feeling stayed with me.

I mean the feeling that there *was* a reason.

I felt extremely alert, as if something might be right out there in the dark, maybe so close that I could even bump into it. And it was so dark in there, and the smell of dead grass and gasoline was so strong, that I guess that's also why I felt a little dizzy and unsteady on my feet.

I reached out my hands like a tightrope-walker so as not to waver back and forth and possibly fall—when all the frickin' lights came on!

I didn't move.

Well, I jerked my head.

I'd never been so surprised to see a room in my whole life.

Really it wasn't much of a room. It was just a dirty basement. Clean, but dirty. I mean, what I saw was *clean* enough, organized enough: these glass cabinets along one far wall that were filled with papers and stuff; various tables and unused furniture, some of it under sheets to keep it from getting too dusty; a lot of gardening stuff hung on a rack and a rider mower with flat tires; a washing machine and a dryer; and some carpets—big rugs, really—rolled up and wrapped in brown paper, stacked like logs on a big shelf a few feet away from me.

The walls were just the reverse side of the building stones, and the mortar sort of curdled out of them like froth, and the floor was stone too, and covered in dust and drops of dried paint.

There were so many other boxes and pieces of sports equipment and various crates of old clothing that I was a bit surprised to see the room being so ordinary. It was like any-body else's storage basement down the hill where I live, where all the houses are filled with so much random junk that if you looked at it long enough, you'd know everything about the family living there without their ever having to say a word to you, because you'd find photos and documents and letters and everything else people have done and used for years, until it's almost like looking at a museum collection about them. Not that I saw anything *too* personal—I mean, it wasn't like the junk at *my* house; it was all just stuff they'd bought and gotten tired of using, but the feeling was sort of the same.

I just couldn't associate this kind of basement with Laura, whose life, as I guess you've gathered, I thought was only fun and really pretty glamorous, but this room kind of revealed that there was a lot of effort behind that, like machinery behind a curtain that keeps the rest of the palace—and I defi-nitely thought of her house as a palace—in perfect shape.

Of course a lot of this is what I can tell you now just in

retrospect, because at the second the lights went on — while seeing the basement so shabby was a bit of a shock — all I could *really* think about was how I might just drop a load in my pants if somebody actually came down the stairs, which was exactly what was happening.

I didn't know if it was her dad or her older brother, Jack, but upstairs one muffled voice said something I couldn't hear, and then this man, Laura's dad or Jack, said in this very tired voice that almost sounded like a snore, "Yeah, I'll get it," and started coming down the stairs.

The stairs were about fifteen feet across from me — this was a *very* big basement; I guess that that makes it at least a *little* glamorous — and I was standing right in the middle of it, right in the clearest, most open visible place, exactly as if I had wanted to just put myself on display.

But that didn't really matter. Because like I told you — like I *had* to tell you — I am good at hiding.

When the lights flashed on, I'll admit I had a sort of subconscious reaction to the room, and I hope it didn't sound too much like a rude judgment, because I wouldn't want you to think I'm casting *aspersions* on Laura's family because they had a less than perfect basement, but really, the first sort of automatic thought that went through my mind was where to hide.

I saw the best place instantly, even while listening to them talking upstairs.

The best place was under the shelf with the rolled-up rugs;

I just sort of instinctively saw that place and picked it without even really trying.

I was still holding my shoes, because I knew they'd make noise and I certainly didn't want to leave any mud tracks on the floor. So without making a sound—and I can scoot just about anywhere without making a sound, especially over a stone floor—I zipped right over to that shelf.

It was a shelf about a yard deep and ten feet long, waist high, attached to the wall stones with some sort of long bracket and held flat by steel cables strung from each end of the shelf to metal bolts stuck in the wall. I got under it really fast, and it hid me perfectly, because first of all, there was a table not too far in front of it that had boxes and household items both on top and underneath, and also because part of the paper wrapper had come undone off one of the rolled rugs, and it hung down almost all the way to the floor like a brown paper curtain.

The craziest thing is that there was a goddamn *bed* behind that paper curtain. It was this long plushy bed of what looked like piled cotton, and it was very soft and a little greasy under my hands. As soon as I was on it, I smelled the unmistakable odor of dog. And then I remembered Laura's dog, this humongous Doberman named Dobey who scares everybody, and I literally prayed to god in my head, *Oh please don't let them be bringing that dog down*—

I stopped praying.

All I did was listen.

He was out there, Jack was. I figured it was Jack because I didn't think Laura's dad would be singing some pop song to himself, this sort of sing-humming that I heard going from one side of the room to the other as he walked around.

And I was right, it was Jack, because I could see out one end from under the shelf, and at one point he came into view under the light hanging from the ceiling over the washing machine, this big, wide-shouldered guy in a Stanford T-shirt. I think he does actually go to Stanford—Laura said so, she said he was a "Stanford man," those were her exact words, and she really sort of bragged about how brilliant he was.

I saw him noodling around in the cabinet next to the washer. I couldn't get a clue about anything he was up to until I saw him drag out an old leather bag and unzip it and look inside and dig his hand through what I thought by the sound must have been papers and then zip it shut and walk off.

Jack.

I guessed he was back a while from school.

Funny enough, I was sort of glad to see him. He had always been a pretty friendly guy. On a couple of occasions he drove Laura and me to the movies and came to pick us up afterward, and also drove us to this roller-rink, where Laura had taught me how to skate. That was the first date we went on, when we skated around in big circles hanging on to each other in an embrace, because if she'd ever let me go, I'd have fallen on my ass and embarrassed the hell out of her. I remembered it perfectly.

So I liked Jack and had a lot of respect for him for being so big at Stanford and playing football and everything, even though to tell you the truth, he was a very privileged guy and knew it. And I really did forgive him for being a bit naturally snooty to me and not actually deigning to look in my direction when he talked; though in all honesty I have to say he had to keep his eyes on the traffic.

I lay there waiting, hoping he'd go up soon so I could breathe again.

But then he did the worst thing.

I have to admit that lying there on that dog bed I was sweating bullets and really feeling pretty frantic and stupid for even being there; I mean, the whole dumb aspect of having come in sort of fell on me all of a sudden like an avalanche. All I wanted now was for Jack to go the hell back upstairs so I could creep out and climb through the window and go home, because by then I'd finally resigned myself to going home and seeing what was up with my dad.

But instead of that, what happened was that Jack walked right past where I was hiding. I even saw his feet in these sort of plush moccasins going right past. His legs scraped against the paper curtain, and then he must have angled around the table, because he stopped for a few seconds at what must have been the sink I'd washed my hands in, and then I heard some squeaky noises and then this sort of vacuum/lever sound that really made my blood run cold. Then he went up the stairs and shut the door.

The lights went out.

I didn't even move.

I listened hard.

And then I heard it.

Five little beeps, and then a long *beeeeep!*

And I was like, *Oh crap.*

I crawled out very quietly. I swear to god I had this sort of dead feeling in me. I kept crawling and didn't even bother to stand until I was near the sink.

Then I stood.

Yep.

Sure enough, the window was shut, the hose no longer hanging down. I could just barely see, along the edge of the right side of the frame, these two rectangular plastic contacts.

The alarm.

I didn't go back to the bed.

Well, not yet.

I stood there wondering.

I can climb pretty fast. I could climb up and open the window. I could be out in, say, ten seconds. Another ten seconds to run across the yard. Then I could get to the alley behind the house. Once there, well, I could hide in another yard or something. It would be easy.

Except one thing.

Jack was on a football scholarship. He was a running back.

I stopped for a second and smiled, wondering just where he'd tackle me. Probably about five feet from the window, because he'd know just which one had been breached—they'd have a sensor board upstairs, I was sure.

Alarms would go off. The roving van would arrive. The woman cop with her hair in a bun would arrive. I'd go to jail. My dad would have to come and get me.

I went back and lay down on the dog bed.

I turned on my back and tried to see the underside of the shelf above me. Finally I did, just the faintest image of the unpainted wood. I reached up and touched it a couple times, almost to remind myself that I was actually there. I wasn't very hungry; although I couldn't remember when I'd last eaten, it must have been hours ago.

My eyes started feeling fuzzy and finally they closed.

Anyways, that's how I came to be hiding in my ex-girlfriend's house.

CHAPTER

SIX

To tell you the truth, I've always been pretty lousy with girls. Going out with them has been difficult for me.

I don't mean I don't like them or anything like that.

I've *always* liked them. I've liked them since I was, like, six years old. I mean I've wanted a girlfriend since I was six. Really.

I probably like them *too* much, because to tell the truth, they drive me a little crazy. You've probably noticed that.

I even like them when they have a cold or a runny nose or when they're just walking down the street. I mean I'm *interested* in girls in general in sort of all the phases of who they are, and not just when they're all dressed up and standing around at some party trying to get noticed.

Actually, it was not entirely correct for me to say that Laura was my first girlfriend, because if you want to just factor in girls in general, she really wasn't. I mean, she was my first girlfriend in *certain* ways, and by that I mean certain uncomfortable and potentially awkward ways that sort of put a lot of pressure on our whole relationship.

I'll tell you what I mean by that in just a little bit, but what I should do first is talk a little about this other girl I know, this girl in my neighborhood named Suzie Perkins, because if I have to say I ever had another girlfriend, it'd be Suzie for sure, except that we were never really romantically involved or anything.

We were *almost* romantically involved, or maybe I should say we certainly *could* have been romantically involved, but the truth is, we were always just friends, and still sort of are, but always, like I said, with a hint of potential romantic involvement, even though in the end it didn't work out that way.

I met Suzie about a million years ago when I was only about twelve, so it's almost like I grew up with her, or at any rate we got to know each other pretty well before we got to be teens and there's all this pressure to start making out, as if when you see a girl and some bell doesn't go off in your head you've got some weird problem, which is a situation that's really pertinent to Suzie and me. I mean really sort of *apt,* and you'll know why later. That hadn't happened yet at all, because when we first met we were almost still virtually just little kids.

It was through that kid I know named Carol that we met, I mean Suzie and me, because Carol was always finding out about new kids in the neighborhood and Suzie had just moved in next door to him, so naturally when she came out in the yard in front of her house my friend Carol—who is a boy, by the way, even though his mom named him Carol, which in certain ways is a very preppy, sort of stand-out name—went out and started to chat her up to find out where she'd moved from and what school she was going to and everything like that.

One thing you've got to know about Carol is that he's actually very weird. He would sometimes lie about who he really was. I mean, he would actually adopt a false *identity* and tell people he had different parents and lived in a different neighborhood and all these other lies, like being a tennis champion, just to impress them and see their reactions. It gave him what he called a *private* satisfaction, and I will say he never did it to scam or cheat anybody; his whole sort of *private* satisfaction was just seeing them believe he was somebody else.

Sometimes we'd be standing around a store or out in a parking lot waiting for his mom after we'd gone to the movies or something, and he'd start a little conversation with somebody passing by—some adult usually, but he was good at this with kids, too—and tell them all about himself, but saying he went to a different school than he really did, and lived in a wealthier area of the neighborhood, or a different neighborhood entirely, or even a different *state,* and people seemed really impressed by him, which was only natural because of all the terrific things he said about himself.

He did it with kids in the neighborhood, too. When a new kid would come along, riding his bike or something, Carol would ask him little questions about whether he was actually *moving* into the neighborhood or was just *visiting* family or friends. And if the kid was just a visitor, and Carol knew he could get away with BSing him without any, you know, future *repercussions,* he'd start his routine. Like if the kid was riding a new bike or hover board or something that was popular, Carol would say to the kid, "Oh yeah, I have one of those." And he'd act very natural and sort of disinterested, but look at the hover board or whatever with sort of squinty eyes, and say, "Mine's a little *better,* though. It has these cool *braking* features I don't see on yours—that lever you can press your foot down on?" By this time the kid would be dying to see what Carol was bragging about, but Carol would sort of shake his head. "No—it's not here," he'd say. "It's up at the cabin in Maine."

That was the thing.

Every time Carol would mention something he had that I knew for a *fact* he didn't have, he'd say it was up at his "cabin in Maine," which he said was on this beautiful lake and surrounded by huge mountains. I knew he was just making it all up—but even if it *had* been real I doubt the cabin would be much to live in, because it'd be crammed floor to ceiling with all the stuff he said was up there that other kids had and he didn't.

Anyways, I don't know if Carol acted weird and did all this stuff when he met Suzie that day. I doubt he did, because like I said, he was really good at asking all these questions to find out whether whoever he was talking to was going to actually live in the neighborhood or not, and seeing as how there was a moving truck and everything, he was undoubtedly aware that she was here to stay. But he asked her a zillion questions anyway, so by the time I showed up in the afternoon he had worked up what you could call a complete *dossier* on Suzie, who he said was sort of skinny like a string bean, with a round face and short black hair cut in bangs and freckles on her face.

"Her mom's divorced," Carol told me about Suzie. We were standing in the street in front of his house and looking at her house on the corner, which still had plenty of unpacked boxes on the porch. He spoke from the side of his mouth and made it all sound very secretive, which he was very good at. So good, in fact, that his mom had managed to get him into a bunch of TV commercials — *spots,* he called them — shunting him off to New York or Hollywood every once in a while, to be in some commercial for cereal or toothpaste. That must be what made him feel so comfortable with lying — and from what I could see was what supported their whole household, because I never saw Carol's mom ever go to work.

His mom was divorced, too, so he winked at me, like he knew something deep about what that meant. "She's okay, but her mom's gross. She weighs, like, six hundred pounds. Kind of makes you wonder, you know?"

"Wonder what?" I said.

He squinted and grinned at me. "Wonder if her daughter will become a whale," he said.

Carol liked figuring everything out about people because he had this very nosy, brassy mom who sort of *primed* him to get all the facts about the people he met. I'm not saying she was nosy just to *judge* people like everybody else around here, but more to see what she could *get* from them, because you always had the feeling she was one of those people who sort of lived by their wits. She was what you'd call a hip mom, and dressed hipper and more casually than the other neighborhood moms —really, I guess, in a more sexy way. Carol called her by her first name, and she did stuff like smoke pot with him once in a while—at least he *said* she did, but he could have been lying. But even if that was a lie, her whole *attitude* and the sort of confidential way she talked to us made her different from any other mom I knew.

Carol looked like his mom, too, like they were peas in a pod, with sandy hair in bangs and freckles and eyes they always squinted at you when they talked, even on cloudy days or when they were *inside* the house—I guess some people just have a knack for doing that, especially people who don't, you know, tell you everything they're thinking. I swear, they were, like, *addicted* to squinting. They even squinted at *each other* when they talked among themselves.

Suzie wasn't there anymore; she'd gone back in next door to eat lunch. Carol and I went and sat inside the big screened-in porch in front of his house — the veranda, he called it — waiting for her to come back. Actually, his place was two houses: a duplex, one side of which various people moved into and out of all the time, which was a very rare thing in my neighborhood. It was sort of a house for transient types; at least that's what my dad called it when I told him Carol lived there.

We sat in big wicker chairs with these dusty flower-embroidered cushions, and Carol went on to tell me that Suzie's mom worked in some job for a contractor downtown, so Suzie was alone most of the time, and that she liked to ride her bike up and down the street a lot, and that she was all set to go to this private girls' school out in some county about fifty miles away, for which she was going to have to be picked up by a yellow bus every morning, even though that detail wasn't particularly relevant right then, because it was just the start of summer, and school for anybody, public and private both, was, like, three months away.

It was about this time that Suzie came back out and I saw her for the first time.

Carol was right about her.

She *was* just a sort of skinny average kid, except that her face was really round and sort of pretty. Her hair was cut in bangs around her face, sort of further setting off the roundness —except that it worked well because her hair was really black. Her skin was very pale and her eyes were this sort of crystal blue with a sparkle that I hadn't seen too many times in other people, except maybe my mom, because she has eyes like that too, and they're the kind of eyes that seem to go very deep because they are so bright, and they give you the impression that the person who has them is very sensitive, but whether that's actually true or not I can't say, because sometimes with my mom the crystal just turns to ice.

But anyways there she was, dawdling in the screen door-way, still eating half a sandwich. She had on this striped shirt like Waldo in the *Where's Waldo?* book, so in truth I'll say she could have looked a little silly, but the odd thing was the way her face and really her whole head didn't go much with her body, which was just this sort of string bean kid's body like Carol had said.

"Hi," she said, smiling at me. "I'm Suzie." And just from the way she said it, I knew immediately she wanted to be friends.

"Hi," I said. "Welcome to the neighborhood."

The best thing about her face was how friendly it looked. She smiled a lot, for one thing—a bright toothy smile between big red lips—and it was pretty hard not to get affected by that smile, because, like those crystal blue eyes, the smile seemed to shine. She seemed like she was always in a really good mood and very friendly, and her voice was friendly too, with a little tinkle of laughter in it.

We did a bunch of things that day, like walking in the woods at the end of the street, and after that, at sunset, just sitting on Carol's porch in the big dusty wicker chairs, drinking iced tea Carol's mom brought out to us.

"Hey — can you show us your house?" Carol asked Suzie, sort of all of a sudden. He was pretty eager to further check out who she was, I could tell.

"Can't," Suzie said. She smiled at him. "My mom's a real stickler about me never bringing anybody inside while she's gone." She sucked on her straw until it bubbled super loud. "So's not to mess anything up," she explained.

I sucked my straw too, just to make the same noise. All Carol did was sit there looking bummed, because I guess he really wanted to check out her house, but he got over it soon enough.

We sat and talked until after dark. And without even trying we all became friends.

I saw her a lot after that. Pretty soon I was seeing her almost every day, because her house was at the bottom of a hill I liked to ride my scooter down, on this sort of secluded street with the houses back behind the trees, where there were never a lot of cars.

Sometimes I found her riding her bike like Carol had said, but the reason she did it was to dry her hair after she'd taken a shower.

I figured this out when once I found her standing in the street with her legs over her bike. I sat on the curb. "I hate using hair-dryers because they always *bake* my hair," she said. "Did you ever notice that? How they just *bake* your hair? I mean until you can *smell* it?"

I told her I understood perfectly, but what I really liked was what she did next, which was big and dramatic, like something I'd never think of doing.

She pedaled way up the street to the top of the hill, turned in a big loop, and soared down yelling, *"Wheeee!"* When she got to the bottom she slammed on the brakes in this terrific skid, right in front of me. We talked for a minute until she got her breath, and then she did it again.

I swear, she did it, like, twenty times. The whole bottom of the street was covered with skid marks by the time her hair was dry. She used to do this all the time, and I loved to watch.

Sometimes Carol was there, and he'd tell us all about what commercial he was up for or already did and what TV star he did it with, or about some political candidate his mother was rooting for, because his mom discussed politics with him a lot, and since both Suzie and I knew nothing about politics, he'd ask us in this sort of condescending way *why* we didn't know anything about the candidate, because it was important to be up on things like that.

But the truth is, I couldn't relate too well to Suzie when Carol was around because the stuff he said sort of hogged the atmosphere. I mean, he had this way—what with his squint and everything—of really just *hogging* the atmosphere, the *whole* atmosphere. I was glad when he started coming around less and less—his mom was always taking him out of town to be in more commercials—but that didn't stop me from coming to see Suzie.

I'm not saying that I stole his friend or anything. It's true that he met her first, but he and Suzie never truly hit it off.

Suzie and I got along really well. I have to admit that the first few times I rode my scooter down the hill I did it sort of accidentally-on-purpose—I mean just to bump into her. But after a few days we were saying to each other that we'd meet there again the next day.

It wasn't long before we'd talk about almost anything, no matter how personal. She told me all about how her dad had left and moved to Cincinnati and the whole ordeal of that, and I told her about my dad and mom and the problems they had sometimes. We'd sit on the curb right next to each other, feeling very close, and I guess we sort of accepted each other as confessional types, because neither of us ever said anything to make the other feel embarrassed or wrong about what we said. I mean, we sort of *sympathized* with each other a lot, because we really did have a lot of stuff—at least *home* stuff —in common.

But the big thing is, we liked each other. We saw each other just as we were and that was all we needed. It was great *not* to hide from her. I guess I felt I could get away with that because her life was so busted up, there was no threat that she'd turn around and judge me. We became pretty close, and sometimes in the evening she'd even come out in her PJs to talk. When her mom called her back in—because her mom had all these *rules* about just when she could go out and *exactly* what she was allowed to do—I'd see her run up onto the porch through the dusk, and I'd wait outside on the street until she showed up at her bedroom window and waved good night down to me.

Now, I won't say I loved her.

But I really, really liked her.

We definitely had feelings for each other, but the amazing thing is that we knew all of each other's dirty little secrets, and it didn't matter. I felt I could tell her anything, like there was no pretense, you know? She didn't hide from me, either. And we didn't have to wear masks and imply things about how rich our parents were or how great we were in school or how cool our lives were in general. I couldn't wear a mask anyway— it wasn't something I was good at doing, faking. You might think I was, because I say I'm good at hiding, but wearing a mask isn't like hiding at all. With a mask, people always know you're right behind it, and they always try to peek through. With hiding they don't see you at all.

After school started, Suzie confided in me all about the problems she had getting along with these nasty girls in her class, and about how much pressure her mom put her under because they couldn't really afford her school on her mom's skimpy salary—this very expensive prep school, it was—so her mom had, you know, these very heavy and extreme *expectations* and everything.

Suzie could tell me anything. And I could tell her anything too, all about how I felt so out of place sometimes, in the neighborhood, I mean, and how I felt we just didn't fit in like other families there, because I hadn't been brought up doing the same stuff that most other neighborhood kids had, and I just couldn't relate to them. And when I told her these things I noticed she would hold my hand.

I would never have thought to criticize or judge her—all I wanted to do was know she was feeling okay and things were decent with her, and I think that's what she felt about me.

Maybe I *was* in love with her but I didn't know it at the time, because when things changed I really got confused.

And things did change.

It happened after two summers, after what I'll say was a pretty blissful time we'd had just hanging out and being friends.

And it wasn't just puberty.

I mean, I guess that's sort of what it maybe boils down to, but that wasn't all of it.

We both went through it at the same time.

And to tell you the truth, at first it wasn't a big deal.

We still saw each other almost every day. We still talked and were close.

But something had happened to her that was pretty incredible, even though I didn't notice it at first.

She became really beautiful.

I mean, she became almost a woman.

How it happened I don't know. I mean, you couldn't tell by looking at her mom how Suzie would turn out, because her mom was really pretty fat. I'd seen her by then, although she wasn't the *whale* Carol and his mom made her out to be —I think they said that out of sheer competitiveness or something. Suzie never got fat. She just really filled out, and whatever tendency she had toward fat, let's just say it all went into the breast area.

That doesn't happen to every girl, you know. Just a few in this right-off-the-bat way.

I guess it really happened gradually, but I hadn't paid attention. She was no longer a skinny kid, and her body now fit her face, but what difference did it make to me? We still talked to each other about everything and I still sat on the curb with my feet on my scooter and watched her ride her bike up and down the hill to dry her hair; that's all that mattered to me, I suppose.

It was the day that Carol came back from a trip to New York that it got ugly. I mean an ugly thing happened.

We were sitting on the porch again, the veranda, all three of us, and I forget how it started, but after bragging to us about some commercial, Carol told some semidirty joke. And then Suzie told one she'd heard at school, and then I did, and we were all laughing, and then we did this wrestling thing we always did, just wrestling one another down until they squirm, and then laughing some more.

But this time I swear Carol had this sort of squinty look in his eyes when he looked at Suzie—I mean an *exceptionally* squinty look—like almost a pissed-off look. I'd noticed it on his face since he'd first seen Suzie that morning. At first he wrestled with me and of course lost because he couldn't beat me in a trillion years, and then he wrestled Suzie down onto this big dusty divan that was stuck against the wall under some windows.

He got her on her back and pinned her arms with his knees so his hands were free, and they were both laughing their heads off, until he raised his hands over her breasts, and I imagine you've gathered from what I said that she had really big breasts by now, and he made his fingers like pincers, and then in this weird voice he started saying, *"Squeezie squeezie squeezie!"* like a frickin' pervert.

She gave up struggling and just stared at his face. I saw her eyes were very hard—I mean the crystal had become icy—and her whole face, which was usually so pale, blushed deep red.

"Get the hell off me," she said.

He rolled off looking like she'd bitten him—I mean embarrassed as hell—and she got up from the divan and straightened her clothes. She said to him, "How dare you do that to me! I thought you were my *friend*."

I'd never heard her voice like that before, so sharp, I mean.

She glared at him, and he didn't say a thing but just sort of looked at the floor. And then she left, just walked out and crossed the yard and went up the stairs to her house and closed the door.

I didn't see her for a week after that.

I saw Carol.

I thought he'd acted like a total moron, but I guess he just felt so embarrassed that he said some pretty nasty things about Suzie to sort of save face. "Jesus," he said. "So she's got a big pair of tits! Is she *uptight* about them? My mom says she's ridiculous. Get *over* it!"

He looked at me with his eyes wide open. I knew he wanted me to agree with him, but I didn't say a thing. It never even seemed to *occur* to him to consider her feelings. I don't know what we talked about next—not much, probably, and I must admit I avoided him for a while after that, like a few weeks. His whole routine had made me sick.

Anyways, the next time I saw Suzie was at a party near her house, down in the woods at the end of the street. I guess her mom was out of town on business or something.

This was one of the first times we'd ever had any beer around. Some kids had raided their parents' stash or gotten their older brothers to buy it for them, I don't know, but all the kids were sitting on this concrete wall that ran along the stream in the woods, and a few of them, the ones with the beer, had dunked it in the stream behind the wall to keep it cold and hide it, even though we were far enough from the street that we could have put it anywhere and not be seen with it unless somebody came walking up really close.

When I arrived it was already dusk. Suzie was there standing around in a crowd of other girls and we said hi and were friendly enough.

But there was a sort of look in her eye when she saw me.

It was the first thing I noticed.

I thought maybe she was a little angry with me. She looked a lot like Carol had the day he came back from New York, this kind of hard, squinty look in her eyes, and later on when we sat next to each other on the concrete wall I noticed the same look.

It was pretty late by then, maybe eleven. We'd both had a few beers, which tasted nasty, and we were pretty much drunk, I guess, because we'd both never had beer before in our lives—at least I hadn't.

We started talking, and her voice was slurred, and I saw for the first time how pretty she was.

More than pretty.

She was totally beautiful, and even though she had beer breath, it still smelled very fresh and nice, and she held her face close to mine, I mean *really* close, and after a few minutes of talking, she put her arm around my back. I thought she did it to keep from falling backwards off the wall. And then she closed her eyes, and her head dropped onto my shoulder.

"Do you mind?" she murmured, right in my ear. "I'm just *sooo* tired." You should have heard her voice—it's like she was cooing.

I just sat there.

I think I sat there for, like, fifteen minutes, frozen.

It's like I was in sort of a daze.

What woke me out of it was this stubby kid in a flannel shirt, Tommy Werks, who was sitting next to me on the other side. I remember he looked over at me with genuine shock in his eyes and said—gasped, really—*"Jesus! I can't believe you!"* and jumped down off the wall to get away from me.

After that Suzie came out of it. She raised her face off my shoulder. "I've got a headache," she said. Then she looked at me sort of sadly, told me good night, and walked out of the woods to the street.

I stayed sitting there.

A few minutes later Tommy Werks came back up. He was a lot shorter than me, but about a year older.

"I can't *believe* you!" he said again. He actually sputtered it, really sputtered, because except for his beady little eyes, his face was all nose and lips. "You *had* her! She was *waiting* for you! Why the hell didn't you *do* anything! You make me *sick!*"

He didn't even wait for me to answer. He just turned on his heel and stomped off through the trees.

I didn't know what to think.

I'm not an idiot.

I sort of knew what had happened.

That day Carol had done the squeezie thing.

That had changed everything.

It was like hanging a sign with ten-foot letters: WE CAN SEE THEM!

Carol, in one fell swoop, had brought all this sex—I mean like a *tsunami* of sex—into our friendship.

Even into mine and Suzie's.

And I don't think that either of us knew what to do about it.

When she had been sitting so close with her face so close, I knew that maybe she wanted me to kiss her.

Or maybe not.

And maybe I wanted to kiss her — or maybe not.

Maybe we really were attracted to each other in that way now.

But I wasn't sure. And I couldn't risk ruining what we had.

So I couldn't just kiss her and stick my tongue in her mouth and feel her up sitting there on that wall. And I *sure* didn't want to do it with everybody else — all the other kids and Tommy Werks especially — standing around and sort of getting their *jollies* seeing us make out. That's just not something I'm particularly into, although I must admit that old Suzie didn't seem like she would mind at all.

I blew my chances with her, as stubby Tommy Werks would say.

That's true.

I still sort of blame Carol. If he hadn't done what he'd done, things wouldn't have been so accelerated. But it happened just like I'm saying.

Anyways, I'm still friends with Suzie.

But that moment never came again. Sometimes I wished it would.

She's still around. Carol is too. It isn't like I stopped being friends with him. And of course I still see him on TV sometimes.

You know, in one way, old Tommy Werks was right.

I really did blow it.

Because one thing you have to know is that if you are

friends with a girl who becomes as incredibly beautiful as Suzie Perkins, you need to keep in mind that there are other boys around.

Lots of them.

Tons of them.

It wasn't a *week* before I saw her on the street walking under the trees with another guy.

And then one night at a party she was tipsy again, and letting this super handsome jock scratch her all over in really inappropriate places—inappropriate for public perusal, I mean. It sort of made me sick, especially how the jerk grinned up at me while he was doing it, as if all he really wanted to do was just show off what he could get away with.

Anyways, by the time I finally met Laura, I had the experience with Suzie under my belt.

I won't say it was a *lot* of experience, but I learned that if you are really great friends with a girl, you have to accept that sex can change everything and might ruin everything. That's another thing my mom told me, and I know it sounds corny and obvious, but when it's actually happening to you, it's not corny at all. I must admit that I found that really hard to deal with. I knew Suzie so well. Had I fallen in love with her, it would have been great.

Or maybe not.

I'll be honest: I couldn't hide around Suzie. I doubt she'd have ever *let* me hide. If we'd fallen in love, I bet we'd have been all over the place, probably making out on every wall in the neighborhood.

Laura had let me hide. She had come looking for me only as far as I wanted her to. But Suzie knew everything about me. I'd *told* her everything until there were no more secrets, but there was no more mystery, either.

I guess I wasn't in love with her.

I don't want to sound stupid, but maybe you can't know everything about the person you fall in love with, at least at first.

Maybe in a way you need to hide.

Maybe it's hiding that makes you feel less awkward.

I've thought a lot about it, and I think it's true.

It's sad, but I think it's true.

CHAPTER
SEVEN

When I woke up I had no idea what time it was.

Early.

I saw sort of bluish morning light coming in where I lay, behind the brown paper curtain.

I didn't even get up. I just listened.

I really had no idea where I was, either.

At least not at first.

I just lay there looking up at the underside of the boards.

The whole thing reminded me of a story I once read in grade school, one of those Edgar Allan Poe stories I'd found in the library, about a guy who's afraid he'll get buried alive because he falls into these weird comas sometimes, so he goes about building this really elaborate tomb that has all these bell pulls and spring-loaded doors and stuff like that, so in case he does ever get accidentally buried, he can just pop right out like a jack-in-the-box. But then he goes on this camping trip with his friends, and of course it rains really hard so they can't sleep in the open, and the only place the guy can sleep is in this sort of coffin-size box in a cabin, and when he wakes up he's forgotten how he got there and he screams his head off, thinking he was buried alive.

Well, I didn't have any bell pulls, so I stayed there, looking up at the wood. I guess I was still pretty drowsy, because I just couldn't get it together.

But then I smelled dog and that did it. I tightened my hands on the plush under me.

It all came back.

At first I was sort of confused, because all that stuff about Suzie was still on my mind. I guess maybe I'd dreamed about it or just thought about it while I was still half-asleep. But when I realized I was in Laura's house—that I had actually sneaked in and fallen asleep on her dog's bed in the basement—I must admit I felt pretty freaked out.

What bothered me most, though, wasn't that I had come in, even though I know it's about the weirdest thing I could possibly have done.

What got me was something hidden in my mind; I was really busy sort of mentally *factoring* some problem I hadn't figured out, a problem that had to do with *both* Suzie and Laura.

I didn't know why I'd thought so much about Suzie,

because to tell the truth, she and Laura had nothing much in common with each other at all. They hadn't even ever *met* each other, because they had never gone to the same school or anything, and girls from The Oaks rarely came down into Ivy Hill, and vice versa.

I don't even think I'd ever *mentioned* Suzie to Laura, because I'm not really into talking about girls to girls—I mean telling them about other girls I had liked—because I don't know what the *benefit* would be, unless I just wanted to make them jealous, and I'm not a big proponent of doing that, and I don't think I'd do it even if a girl asked and was curious about other girls I'd been into. I didn't even *know* Laura when I had hung out with Suzie, because I hadn't even met her yet.

Still, there seemed to be some sort of connection between them in my mind, some sort of very close *connection*, which I know sounds crazy, and I really thought it was, so I just sort of stopped my mind from thinking, really just told it to shut up for a little while, and I leaned up on the dog bed and listened.

There wasn't any sound upstairs.

No footsteps or noises.

I didn't even hear Dobey up there, which sort of surprised me, because dogs are usually pretty good at sniffing out intruders.

All I could think about was how I wanted to get the hell out of there.

I got up very quietly and went over to where I'd stood

the night before, right in front of the sink. I looked around. Certainly nothing had changed; there was no special evidence that anyone other than Jack had come downstairs during the night or anything.

I raised my leg over the sink and very carefully climbed up on it until I was on my knees. I held on to the faucet for balance. It had two spigots attached to it, on one of which was the attachment fixture for the hose that had been strung out the window, but that Jack had disconnected the night before.

I looked outside. All I could see was a green glow under the still sort of bluish morning light, and a bit of the yard through the bushes I'd hidden behind last night before I climbed in.

Kneeling there like that I realized I was pretty hungry. And I had to pee. But not too badly, thank god, because if I did I'd have to do it in the sink and then I'd have to turn the faucet on, and it would make noise all throughout the house.

And really, what if somebody upstairs just happened to come downstairs and caught me peeing in their sink?

So I sort of gave up on the idea of relieving myself—at least until the coast was clear.

The window was locked. I saw the lock, just a little plastic lever shaped like an L. No key or anything. I could open it, for sure. It would of course set off the alarm. But this time I might just make it. Climbing out in the daylight would be easier. I'd be able to make it to the back alley fast, and from there I could just hide somewhere; that would be extremely easy for me.

They might not catch me, and because there was no evidence I'd been inside, there was even a possibility they might just think it was a system malfunction or something, and never even realize I'd been there.

I thought about doing it for a second. It sort of made me smile. Even Jack wouldn't be fast enough to catch me—he'd have to get dressed, for one thing, or at least put his pants on. I think it was imagining him rushing to get into his pants that made me smile.

But I just couldn't see waking them up that way. It'd be too much of a shock for them to have to bolt out of bed thinking there were intruders in the house. Anyways, I didn't even have my shoes on.

I climbed down and got my shoes out from behind the curtain. I checked to see how wet they were; they were still a bit damp. Dirty, too, even though I'd wiped a lot of the mud off. I couldn't put them back on without leaving tracks, I was sure.

I really didn't know what to do, and right then, like a very distant chime, I heard an alarm clock go off.

Oh boy, I thought.

As fast as I could, I crept under the curtain and lay back on the bed.

I can't tell you how badly I needed to pee. It was like that alarm clock had sort of *activated* it.

I lay there listening, and in no time the upstairs was full

of noises. Not that the floor creaked or anything like it would have at my house, because back there if you were down in the basement — or cellar, really, because I don't want to, like, *enno-ble* my house to make it sound anything like Laura's — you'd have heard, like, the whole floor creaking and shrieking like an earthquake was on its way.

All I heard were the little thumps of footsteps, and it was pretty easy to distinguish, by what you could call almost the weight of the sound of the footsteps, who was walking around up there, which was obviously Laura's dad and her brother, Jack, because they had, you know, more thump to them, and then Laura's mom, with a little less thump, but I must admit certainly *some* thump, and then last of all Laura, who of course had almost no thump at all, because she's actually quite graceful.

"I used to study gymnastics," she had told me one night when she was baby-sitting. We lay piled on the sofa in the game room, taking a break from making out. "Since I was five. I guess I'm okay at it."

That's all she ever told me about it, and I was surprised she downplayed it, because she really did always brag about almost everything else, her family especially. But I knew she was very good, because she used to do these crazy flips in the park when we'd go for walks, and she was actually *incredibly* good at it, at least in my opinion. She'd just sort of grin at me and say, "Hey, watch this!" and then *whoosh,* she'd run over the grass and suddenly, she'd literally be *upside down* in the air, and then back on her feet again like she'd just stepped off a curb or something. I must admit I was always very impressed by that, and these were also some of the few times that I ever saw her really seem to feel good, like she'd done something special that only she could do.

Now, you probably won't believe it, but all I wanted to do was get out of that basement.

First of all, I will admit it was actually very exciting being down there on the dog bed and knowing Laura was upstairs. I mean, I can't deny that.

But despite all the undeniable excitement, I was worried.

I really did begin to worry pretty badly, because despite everything I've already said about how it would be impossible to ever be unhappy in this sort of house and how all your problems would just be sort of fun, the truth is, I didn't want to know. I didn't want to know that maybe everything wasn't perfect in this house.

I didn't want to *eavesdrop,* for one thing, because I knew how terrible that would be to do, and my only real wish was that Jack had forgotten to shut the window and turn on the alarm, so I could just climb the hell out of there.

Because to tell you the truth, I didn't want to be disappointed. And I had the feeling I would be.

I mean, I knew I had all these kinds of *illusions* about

Laura, because for one thing, I totally loved her, and for another thing, she *wanted* me to have them.

She had, I must admit, always bragged about how rich her family was, especially her dad, who she said managed a hedge fund, and I for one, not being much up on financial matters, really had no idea what that even was and at first thought it was maybe some kind of joint bank account for landscapers.

But she let me know that actually it meant he was, like, the big cheese for a whole huge group of investors and sub-investors and sub-subinvestors, and the whole thing sounded so complicated that I never really could get my head around it, except that she said, "He makes about two million a year."

That part I understood.

I was like, "Wow. Your dad makes two million a year."

And she said, "He's buying a house in Buenos Aires next year. He does a lot of building down there with developers. My dad's from Argentina, you know."

We had been standing by a fence in a park, the one by my old elementary school. It was twilight. I don't know why, but she seemed sad. I mean, here she was bragging about her dad and how rich they were, and telling me all the details, but it didn't really seem to make her smile. If anything, she seemed a little angry.

But she didn't stop there. She went on and told me about their boat, called the *Esmeralda* or something, which sounded like a really great boat with, like, six sleeping cabins in it, and how she was going to get a Jet Ski, which was certainly something that I'd always wanted.

I asked her if she would let me ride it.

She said, "Sure. If you can get to Buenos Aires."

That crack made her smile a little, which she almost never did when she was around me, so I was glad she'd made it. Like the times she did the flips, I really liked to see her happy, even if this time it was at my expense.

What's weird about this is you might think, you know, that by making that sort of joke—because I obviously would never be able to get myself down to Buenos Aires unless I walked, and that would take probably five years—she was being mean to me and maybe didn't like me. But this whole time she was holding my hand, really holding it tightly, as if her life depended on it. It actually even *hurt* a little, and I could feel her fingernails sticking into my palm. Holding her hand made me feel so glad I was with her, even more than seeing her face, which I thought looked so beautiful in the dusk, with those liquid eyes she had looking at me and seeming to search me for something without ever finding it, but *hoping* to find it, and her round face that I thought was so beautiful and her shiny brown hair that fell across her forehead like a wing.

Just then I heard water coming through pipes, not loud

and obnoxiously like in most houses, but pretty smoothly. I figured somebody had used the toilet or turned the water on in a sink.

I heard voices.

I had said I didn't want to eavesdrop, but I must admit that a sort of intense curiosity was building up in me. I really wanted to hear what they were saying. I had to get up and cross the room. I mean, lying on the dog bed, I knew I wasn't going to learn too much about anything.

I know I said I was afraid of wrecking my illusions about her; I know I sort of said that.

But just hearing her voice again would be great.

So I got up and went to the stairs.

I had to kind of hold my crotch when I walked. That's because I still had to pee. Already in my mind I was sort of factoring what I'd do when everybody left. I *hoped* they were all going to leave—that was something I figured I might find out if I listened in a little. I certainly hoped nobody was staying home for the day. Can you imagine what the headline would say if somebody happened to open the basement door? "BOY HOLDING HIS CROTCH CAUGHT IN EX-GIRLFRIEND'S HOUSE."

Boy, oh boy.

But I was holding it just because I had to pee—don't get any dirty ideas.

I got up the stairs without too much difficulty, a step at a time. And when I was just behind the door I leaned forward and listened.

They were all getting breakfast ready. I figured the kitchen must have been right behind the door where I was standing, because I heard the sink and plates clinking and the usual breakfast stuff like that. Laura's dad was there, which was pretty unusual because she'd told me he traveled constantly and was never around that much. She actually sort of bragged about how much he flew, and how sometimes he did it on this private jet that was owned by his company on some kind of weird private jet time-share that I couldn't ever understand anything about except that it sounded extremely glamorous.

Anyways, he was talking in Spanish, actually not talking but sort of yelling, though not in an angry way, because he had to talk over his wife, Laura's mom, who was talking even louder than he was. And in the background Jack was banging around with something made of metal, maybe a frying pan or something like that, and he was answering his mom with these little monosyllabic answers when she asked him, rapid-fire, "Have you packed your bags? Did you take your medicine? Did you put the brace on your foot? Well, *did* you?"

I didn't quite get that last part, because in the basement he hadn't limped or anything, but I guessed maybe he'd banged up his foot being such a hotshot running back for the Stanford team.

I was sort of getting an idea here of the family dynamic. I must admit it wasn't anything like I'd thought. I mean, at my house, to tell the truth, everybody is always sort of still exhausted when we wake up and we all kind of slog around and practically bump into one another just trying to stay on our feet. But here there was this sort of frenzied panic, and nothing like the sort of cozy, loving family scene I'd imagined, with everybody sitting around the table like in a cereal commercial.

But what was worst was that every few seconds all I heard was her mom yell, *"LAURA!"*

She yelled it super loud—I mean earthshakingly loud —because I guess Laura had gone back upstairs and was still dawdling in bed or something. You'd figure yelling once was enough, but her mom must have thought she was deaf or something, because a second would pass and then there'd come another big blast: *"LAURA!"* I mean, I think she yelled it, like, *ten* times, and after yelling it she would say to Jack or to her husband these little needling comments about Laura and her *habits*—I mean these sort of nasty little *comments* that she said almost to herself, and I'm not even going to say what they were, because I hated hearing them.

When Laura finally did come down, she had barely said good morning when her mom really just sort of jumped on her. "What was *taking* you so long? You know your brother has a *flight* this morning! You only think of yourself, young lady! We are a *family* here, unless you don't *know* that. *Do* you know it? Have you *forgotten?*" Her voice sounded very sharp and unfriendly. And in the meantime, Laura's dad wasn't even paying attention and never broke in to come to her *defense* or anything; he was off somewhere in the background talking Spanish really fast on the phone, totally oblivious to what was happening between Laura and her mom.

Jack, he couldn't have cared less either, except that every once in a while he'd say something like "Hey, Laurs, can you toss me that juice?" or "Laurs, spin me that butter, will ya?"

I mean, I got her mom's point about making everybody late, and it's certainly something I've been guilty of plenty of times at my house, but really her mom sort of *jabbed* at her when she spoke, and I couldn't stand hearing her. I knew she was in a panic to get Jack to the airport, but she really did sound a little mean, and maybe more than a little. And to tell the truth, she didn't even give Laura much time to answer, because obviously Laura hadn't exactly jumped at what Jack was making in the frying pan and had grabbed something else to eat, and her mom just went at her again, saying, "Are you really going to *eat* that? Don't you *remember* you have an eating disorder? Do you want to be *fat*—is that what you *want,* young lady? Now that you *quit* gymnastics, is your *ambition* to be *fat?*"

By this time, even though I had to pee like a racehorse and was literally squirming on the top step standing on one foot, I was starting to get pretty upset. I don't want to disrespect her mom or anything, but I was like, *God almighty, what a bitch.* I mean, here she is in this incredible house, and she has literally the most beautiful girl in the *entire world* for a daughter—at least that's my personal opinion—and all she can do is say this nasty panicked junk, and Laura obviously can't even answer except to sort of mutter *sure* once in a while, and *yes ma'am,* in such a quiet way that I could hardly hear her beautiful voice.

I was totally shocked. Because the big thing is that when she was with me, Laura had done nothing but *compliment* her mother, just like with her dad. I mean, she complimented and praised her all the time. She even *bragged* about her, saying how she was so into exercise and health food and organics and yoga and meditation. I mean, she would literally sit me down and *lecture* me on her mom's good points, like maybe I should take notes for my personal enrichment. And the truth is that whenever I'd complain about my parents, which, though I hate to say it, was probably like the main staple topic of everything I ever had to say, or at least close to it, Laura would sort of roll her eyes and look at me like my parents having any problems really had to be in the final analysis *my* fault, and what I should do is clean up my act and not be so disrespectful because of, you know, how much *effort* it took to raise a kid and all that sort of stuff. Which was exactly what Laura's mom talked about next, saying, "We wouldn't have to be in *such a hurry* if we didn't have to drop *you* off for school, and with your *grades* where they are, I don't see why we go on *paying* that tuition! Don't you *care* what we do for you, young lady? Don't you *appreciate* it?"

I'd had enough. I really couldn't stand it anymore.

I mean, I swear to god. I hoped it was just an off day.

It probably was.

It had to be. I was sure of it.

I went back downstairs.

I felt pretty lousy. But even though I was, like, really, *really* mad at Laura's mom, I want you to know that I still didn't pee in her damn basement sink.

I waited.

For, like, twenty minutes, I waited.

Then I heard them all leave. Through the basement wall I heard them in the garage attached to the house, and I heard their car drive off, and after that I was alone.

CHAPTER

EIGHT

N ow, I'm sure you're going to believe me when I say that the first thing that came into my mind after I heard them leave was, *This is my opportunity to get out of here.*

And I would have.

Really.

I mean, after hearing what went on in the kitchen I was certainly ready for it. I didn't like what I'd heard at all.

But more than just not liking it, it had totally confused me.

I won't say it *contradicted* what I'd expected, because that's not how I looked at it.

Had it been a contradiction, I just would have heard a bunch of morose voices, or no voices at all, and not the happy loving family scene I'd anticipated, and that would have been just a simple contradiction.

But that wasn't it.

What I'd heard was the whole family *dumping* on Laura.

Or ignoring her.

And I was surprised.

Totally surprised.

Had it just been like a game of opposites and they all hated each other or acted coldly to each other, I would have just been wrong and felt like an idiot, which in truth wouldn't have been hard for me to feel, because I already felt like a total and complete idiot for just still being there.

But what I heard I had no precedent for, if you get what I mean. Laura had always talked about her family as if they were the greatest people in the world.

But great people don't treat their daughter like that.

And that's when a certain thought came to me.

I hardly know how it all added up in my mind, but they say the mind is always working, you know, and sort of *factoring* all these different thoughts and putting them together until they make sense, so right about then I sort of put a bunch of those thoughts together, and bingo, something made sense.

I got an answer to a question I'd always asked myself about her.

Because I'd *always* had a question about Laura, especially when I had believed, and I really, really had believed, all the wonderful things she'd said about her family. And I was sure, *sure,* that getting the answer to my question was, even though you'll think I'm crazy for saying it, part of the reason why I'd come in the house in the first place.

The question was, *What the hell does she see in me?*

I know a lot of guys ask themselves this same question. I mean, especially with your first real girlfriend. You look at her and see this beautiful girl who could have any guy she wants, so you sort of have to ask it—I mean, circumstances sort of *compel* you to.

And I never knew the answer. Until now, when I was sitting at the bottom of her basement steps and staring up at the hopper window, wishing to hell I hadn't heard those five ominous beeps, followed by a long *beeeeep,* right before they left the house to get in their car.

I can honestly say that that was the question I asked myself about her the night when we first met.

I'm still amazed we actually *did* meet, because at the time I was doing one of my greatest performances of hiding that I'd ever managed to pull off, and was quite certain that I couldn't possibly be noticed by anybody.

I was at this party I really shouldn't have been at, thrown by this guy named Walton Roberts, called Biff by his friends for some completely incomprehensible reason, and his parents must have been out of town, because with what was going on in his house when we arrived—my friend Carol and me, we were back to hanging out a lot together then—I knew from the start that no parent in their right mind would ever allow it.

To be really exact, I would never have even been able to get into the party in the first place except for Carol, because he'd gone to the same Catholic middle school as Biff, before Biff went off to be a big shot at Ivy Hill Prep, which is the most exclusive school in my neighborhood, and those guys at Prep never, *ever* associate with anybody like me who goes to Ivy Hill Public; it would be like some kind of *heresy* for them even to allow themselves to be *seen* with a kid like me.

So you can imagine how uncomfortable I felt in this huge house, in The Oaks, of course, and really just about five blocks from Laura's place, and you can probably believe, when I looked through the crowd—and the whole house was incredibly crowded with about a zillion kids, just *swarming* with them —that I felt totally out of place and uncomfortable, and when I say uncomfortable, I mean like triple-root-canal-dentist's-office uncomfortable.

All I could say to Carol, when I wasn't just trying to steady myself and not be knocked over by the crowd, was, "Hey, Carol, why don't we just get out of here?"

He looked at me with a screwed-up face like I was nuts, and yelled, "C'mon, we just showed up!" He had to yell because the crowd was so loud.

I didn't even know how to answer him. I just wanted to vanish.

"Ease up, bro!" Carol said. "This party's *epic!* Stop flipping out and get *into* it!"

"Yeah, right," I muttered.

All around me were hundreds of kids I had nothing in common with. First of all, they all dressed better than me, with super expensive stuff, especially this certain sort of flannel coat they all wore back then but wouldn't be caught dead in now that sort of felt like a comforter. It wasn't even very cold then. I mean, it was already March and things were starting to warm up, but they were wearing these coats anyways just for show, and I will say that the whole party had this sort of serious B.O. problem almost like a mist in the air, but nobody seemed to mind.

I just stood there like a pillar.

I didn't talk.

There was no point in my even *trying* to talk to anybody, because just from what I overheard about sports and travel and driving their new cars, I knew in advance I didn't have much to add to what was being said, except to, like, *display* myself as the most unimpressive person at the party, because I wasn't much involved with any of that sort of stuff and never had been. Anyways, just *hearing* was tough, because Biff had hired this DJ and the music was crazy loud. He was stamping around, I mean Biff, either holding court over all his jock friends in a corner of the room or jumping up and yelling because somebody had knocked over a glass cabinet or something, and so he would come bolting forward to rectify the problem in this really loud, bossy, super authoritative way, as if the person who knocked it over had made the biggest error in the world. Which I thought was kind of stupid, because really when you got down to it, any damage would have been Biff's own stupid fault for throwing the party in the first place.

To be honest, I felt like I'd landed in a nest of alien beings, and even though Carol was keeping up the patter with about a hundred people he knew because he had gone to school with them, I was just standing there, almost pretending I was like some sort of astronaut who'd landed on a planet inhabited by bizarre alien beings I had nothing in common with whatsoever.

And that's when I saw her through the crowd.

She was looking at me.

She was talking to somebody else—a big guy in one of those coats I told you about—but her eyes were turned to *me*.

When I looked, she looked away.

But I kept looking, and she looked back.

Then Carol, who as you've probably gathered never misses anything because he's been, like, *primed* by his mom to catch all the little details, said, "That girl likes you."

I said the great and famous "No, she doesn't."

He talked from the corner of his mouth and looked askance at her from the corner of his eye so she couldn't tell he was watching her. I was impressed by that.

"Uhh, yes she does," he sort of muttered right in my ear. "And, uh—here she comes!"

He looked past me and grinned when he said that, and made this little laugh in his throat he always did when he knew he was completely right about something and had another reason to believe he was totally clever.

I just stood there.

Because he was right.

She *was* coming over.

She was moving through the crowd, and when she passed people, she'd look at me.

How was this possible? With my nonspeaking pillar routine I was supposed to be utterly unnoticeable.

But not to her.

She came walking up, and when she was right in front of me, I was really surprised at how short she was, because I swear she'd looked like a giant coming through the crowd.

"Hi there," she said. "I'm Laura. I think I've seen you around before, maybe at the grocery store."

Now, something weird happened.

It's kind of hard to say just what it was.

We actually got along with each other.

I don't mean to say that our first conversation went

smoothly. It didn't. There were plenty of gaps. But Carol always made up for that. He could toss in talk to keep things going about subjects I knew nothing about.

I told her my name, and she asked where I went to school, and I told her, even though I knew it would wreck everything, but it didn't wreck anything—she just nodded like she'd heard a fact. And like I said earlier, she had this bottle of lotion, and she was putting it on her nose, so I asked her what it was for. "Dry skin," she said. Her eyes were, like, studying me. I saw how deep and dark they were, like pools. My breath caught for a second. She said, "Sunburn. It peels, you know? I spent too much time in the sun in the Bahamas over spring break."

I had nothing to say to that, but Carol did. It turned out he already knew her a little, and they talked about the Bahamas for a while because he'd been there too, but even when she talked to him she was looking at me, with this kind of curious, serious look.

She never smiled.

Or even grinned.

I will say that neither of us ever got goofy or laughy— we just sort of kept looking at each other. And she told me a bit about her family, which impressed me a lot, and I told her about mine, and she gave these little nods to everything I said, still looking at me, right in my eyes.

Something was happening in my mind. I didn't know what it was. It felt warm, almost hot. I couldn't really think straight. I was amazed. I mean, I was amazed I could say anything to her at all, but the truth is, I had no trouble, not at first. But even with this feeling I didn't understand—this new feeling she was *making* me feel just by talking to me—I felt sort of weird, because I was learning something about myself.

She had looked like an alien too.

I'd thought that.

I admit it.

She really had.

I'd sort of made her that way in my mind along with all the other kids at the party, because I'd assumed she had nothing in common with me, like I said.

But as I looked at her face, she made these little *expressions*. Little winces, and she pursed her lips now and then, really listening to me and trying to follow what I said—I mean trying to get *something* out of it, despite the fact that what I was saying really wasn't all that much, and there was that noise all around us I already told you about.

She was *not* an alien.

In her face I saw such warmth and beauty and sadness and humanity that I felt like a fool for having ever seen anything else there.

What I mean is that suddenly—or maybe it was more like *gradually*—all this humanity, this huge *ocean* of humanity, sort of flooded up in her face, and it was all directed at *me*.

I couldn't believe it.

I was speechless.

I mean seriously, I began to find it really difficult to talk.

I can honestly say that when I saw that happen I fell madly in love with her.

We stood there a few more minutes. I can't remember what we discussed. I *did* talk, but barely. I'd never been so distracted by anything in my life as I was by her face.

Then she said, looking between Carol and me, "Well, it's late. Are you boys going to walk me home?"

Carol said we would.

If there's one thing I'll never forget as we walked through the dark to her house, it was that I could feel her walking beside me. I'd never felt that before with anybody. But I swear I always, *always* felt it with her. Carol was walking on my other side and I couldn't feel him there at all, but with Laura it was like I could *feel* this incredible warmth just coursing through her, and I felt it in myself, too.

I'm not trying to say that we were somehow *connected*, but I couldn't really put it any other way. I think even if I'd closed my eyes I would have felt her near me. I didn't feel cold even though it was dark and this sort of chilly wind had started —which I guess explains everybody's coats at the party. She wore one too, a blue one that looked truly great on her, and to tell you the truth, I could see now that it was a very nice coat, and I would have probably bought one for myself if I could have afforded it.

But I never felt cold, even though the air was getting there and was scented, I noticed, by all the trees that stood around us, throwing big shadows on the quiet houses.

We talked about her school play. She was a junior and her play was coming up on Saturday.

I hate to sound stupid, but I didn't really know what to say.

Finally I said, after she'd waited about ten seconds, "Can I come? I really want to see it."

And that's when she smiled, her first smile. Never in my life did I feel I'd asked so brilliant a question.

She said I could. She said she would really like that.

Then she stopped.

She looked aside, and just like that she ran across a dark yard to a big dark house and went up some stairs and turned.

She looked back at me. "Well, good night."

I just stood there.

She didn't move.

Carol managed to prod my back.

"She wants you to kiss her!" he whispered impatiently. "Go over there! And get her phone number, you moron!"

It struck me he was right.

So I went across the yard.

It took courage.

She leaned down from the stairs and we kissed very lightly. I remember her face coming close to mine. I will never forget it. I asked for her number and she wrote it on my palm.

When we were walking again, Carol said, "Man, you almost blew it! Couldn't you see she was really *into* you? Why can't you *talk* to her? You always talked with Suzie! What's up with this?"

I couldn't answer at first. It all seemed too good to be true. I mean, the *question* was already occurring to me. Maybe not in words yet, but I had this crazy *feeling*.

What does she see in me?

But I couldn't tell Carol that. He wouldn't understand.

I looked at him. "I don't know," I said. "I really don't know."

He seemed very frustrated with me. I mean, for a second he looked as disgusted as Tommy Werks; his whole face sort of squeezed, and he shook his head.

Then his face sort of cleared. It emptied. Another look came into it, sort of curious and sympathetic—I mean as sympathetic as Carol could look, because sympathy wasn't really his strong point.

He said, "Maybe you just don't believe it." He looked at me with narrowed eyes, squinting, of course, almost like he was studying me. "Well, come here. You've got to see something."

We ran back to the party. It took about five minutes. I'd sweated a lot without even noticing and I thought I might catch a cold, but I didn't care. I felt so weirdly awake. I felt like I'd woken up for the first time in my life, and that Laura had woken me. I don't know how else to put it.

We passed the party. The house was still lit up. Carol kept running and I followed right on his heels.

He stopped next to this car parked about a block away. It was really nice, a new Tesla that was all black and gleamed under the streetlights.

He was out of breath and bent over for a second, totally winded. Then he stood straight and put his hand on the hood of the car. "See this? It's her dad's car," Carol said.

"What do you mean?" I said.

"She *drove* here! But she didn't *say* she did, so you could walk her home, 'cause you don't have a car! She didn't want to *embarrass* you. Do you *get* me?"

"Yeah," I said. "Yeah."

He shook his head and grinned. "Man, I've heard of a *daze*, dude, but this is —"

"I love her," I said.

I didn't mean to say it. It just came out.

For a second Carol just looked at me.

Then he smiled.

I swear, despite all that squeezie stuff, he could be all right.

"Well, call her. Let me know what happens."

"Sure," I said.

"You *will* call her, right?"

"Sure," I said.

He grinned and ran away into the dark.

I stood there alone, watching him disappear up the street past the house where kids now were pouring out over the bright lawn, leaving, saying goodbye to Biff in the doorway.

I turned toward home, walking down the hill to my house, which I swear looked like a shack compared to the places up there.

My parents were asleep. I went up all the narrow stairs and got in bed. My room was on the third floor. Everything was quiet. I sat up in bed with a light on, staring at clothes I'd tossed on the floor of my room.

I was scared.

I was very happy, but very scared.

The question had already occurred to me, like I said.

I lay in bed for an hour thinking about it.

Repeating it.

What does she see in me?

I couldn't tell; it seemed impossible.

I knew she saw *something,* but I didn't know what it was.

She was so open, so bold, so free and beautiful.

I was all closed up and hidden.

But now I knew.

Sitting in her basement, I knew.

After what I'd heard in the kitchen, I knew.

What did she see in me?

She saw I was *hiding.* And that means she saw *me.*

I'd crawled back onto the dog bed, to once again stare

at my favorite boards. I smiled. My own analytic abilities impressed me a lot, sure. But what I really marveled at was how perceptive *she* was, because that night at the party, I seriously doubt that anyone else there had seen me at all, or would ever remember I'd even been there, Biff included.

So I felt pretty good for a while.

But I didn't feel *too* good.

I would have, but the truth is, another question came up, which didn't feel too good at all.

Had I ever seen her?

CHAPTER

NINE

I sat up on the dog bed and got my shoes. They were practically dry now.

The house was totally empty.

The only sound I heard was Dobey. He was up there for sure, sort of loping from room to room. I heard his paws thumping around, and a bit of his neck chain sort of dragging over the floor, because he wears this adjustable neck chain for a collar—I guess it's called a choker—and when it isn't adjusted properly it hangs really loose in this big loop, which of course tightens up in a second after you put a leash on it.

I put my shoes back on after making very sure they were totally clean, and I lay back on the bed. Believe it or not I hadn't even peed yet. I felt I barely had to. All that needing to go so badly must have been nerves, because now I definitely felt okay and really had no urge to go anywhere near the sink.

I just lay there listening to Dobey and trying to get my thoughts straight about exactly what I had to do.

I knew Dobey pretty well. He was big.

I mean *very* big.

Some Dobermans are sleek like greyhounds and very shiny black and brown, but Dobey was that other kind of Doberman, the really humongous kind, with fur that's still very short but sort of grayish black and not shiny at all, and with so much muscle bulging under his skin that his whole body sort of *undulates* when he walks because you know he weighs at least one hundred twenty pounds.

I mean he was *huge*.

But he was pretty nice. Laura had walked him plenty of times when we were together, and he'd certainly gotten used to seeing me.

So I won't say I was afraid of him attacking me.

Or at least, not that afraid.

I mean, whenever I'd seen him, Laura was always there, and he was on a leash and got plenty of chances to sniff me out, which I must say is pretty embarrassing, especially when you've first met a girl and her dog starts gouging his snout really hard right between your legs. But Laura didn't seem to even notice; I guess she was used to it. And he never bit me or growled at me. I guess he thought I was okay. He never even got bugged when I put my arm around Laura or held her hand, and some dogs, you know, will get pretty touchy about that sort of thing and go off half-cocked if you aren't careful with their masters.

How he would react to just seeing me alone, though, I didn't really know.

Of course, he probably knew I was already in the house.

I mean, with these dogs, and especially a dog like a Doberman that has such a long nose and can probably smell your sock when it's five miles away, you can't really hide much, unless you get into water, I guess.

Now you're probably getting the idea here—by my talking so much about whether Dobey would be happy to see me —that I'd sort of formed a plan to go upstairs into the house.

Well, you're right.

I won't talk about the morals of it right now, because I figure that whatever assessment you've made about my character is probably sort of set in stone by now, and that this going-up-into-her-house idea that I had has sort of *cemented* your mental picture of me, which was probably never too terrific in the first place.

I'll just focus on the technicalities.

First of all, I knew the alarm was turned back on. Like I said, I heard it beep right before they all left to get in the car out there, probably Laura's dad's nifty Tesla, which I must say is a pretty amazing car. So again I had thought about the hopper window, but come on, if I went out of that, you know the sort of trouble I'd be in.

Because think about it.

These people—Laura and her dad and her whole family —have wads of cash, and they undoubtedly got the whole she-bang when they opted for home security, and that means video.

Inside and out.

I mean even out in the yard.

And that made me think how lucky I was, because probably it was infrared like in some spy movie, and even last night they could have seen me, if it had been turned on. If not Laura's family in the house, then the guy paid to watch the video monitor in his office at whatever security outfit they bought the stuff from. This whole neighborhood security network would be alerted, and neighborhood patrols would come by the second I tripped the system.

They wouldn't have motion sensors—I was sure of that. Dobey would set them off.

Still, I had to be careful.

So what I was thinking was, yes, I needed to go upstairs.

This was my plan A.

I needed to go up, make friends with Dobey if possible, avoid any and all video cameras, find the alarm control, locate the code that was undoubtedly written right near it—because nobody can ever remember those sorts of codes and they write them in the stupidest places—enter it, and leave.

Or plan B.

Go upstairs, make friends with Dobey, avoid the video, if unable to find said code, wait in a closet or something until somebody comes home, and try to sneak out when the house is again full of people.

I must admit I preferred plan A.

Except for one thing.

I thought maybe, just before leaving, I'd take a look around.

Now you think I'm a creep.

But I have to admit that I was thinking about exactly that —I mean looking around—and not feeling too good about it, because I really did know it was sort of a creepy idea, and an actually creepier thing to do—I mean, you know, sneaking around your ex-girlfriend's house when she's not even there.

Believe me, I really did think it was creepy.

But after hearing all that talk in the kitchen, something had sort of happened in my mind. I felt I had never *seen* Laura for who she really was; in fact, I was sure of it. So I felt pretty curious to get to know a little more of what she was all about, which I might learn if I managed to leave through the upstairs and got to actually see the inside of her house for a second.

I mean just a *second*.

Okay. I am a creep.

But you know how much in love I was with Laura and

how beautiful and wonderful I thought she was and every-thing. And I must say that being in her house and hearing her upstairs talking had sort of *reactivated* my feelings for her—I mean these feelings that I'd worked really hard to sort of *sub-due* ever since she'd broken up with me. I don't want to sound pathetic, because I want you to know I really had made quite an effort to accept it when she broke up with me because I was "just a boy" and was not ever going to "accomplish anything important" in my life like her mom said, or at least was *poten-tially* not ever going to accomplish anything important in my life.

Now, I know there's nothing worse than loving a girl who doesn't want you anymore. We all know how gross that kind of love is, and degrading and disgusting and weird—I mean, especially a girl who has just grown up, I mean *matured,* because they can feel very sensitive and uncomfortable about things like that. My mom told me all about it, and I must say I sort of got her point completely.

I knew Laura didn't love me anymore.

I *accepted* that.

I had to just *get over it.*

But all these experiences I'd had sort of *concentrated* my feelings; I mean sort of *reactivated* them, like I said.

The truth is, I had the sudden feeling I'd never even really *known* Laura.

I know that sounds crazy, because for a while we were together almost every day, and we kissed thousands of times, and she even let me get slightly intimate with her when she baby-sat, and I told her I loved her at least a thousand times. And god only knows how many times I said she was wonderful and beautiful—hopefully fewer than I seem to remember.

But being in her house and hearing what I'd heard had really gotten me thinking. I'd figured out that answer, for one thing—she saw I was hiding, and she saw me. And the answer gave me that other question, about whether I'd ever seen her at all.

And that question really bugged me.

Because I hadn't.

I knew I hadn't.

She'd seen *me*, all right. The first night we met. She saw me when I was hiding in the middle of that room, and that really blew me away.

But I never knew *why* she saw me. I didn't know what *value* it could possibly have for her.

At the time it just seemed like some freak accident or really just a mistake. But now I thought I knew, or at least had an *inkling*, you know, that I *might* know, because of all that nasty talk I heard coming from her mom, which had sort of given me certain ideas.

So, do you know why I thought she saw me?

You know why I thought she could?

Because she was good at hiding too.

I got up from the dog bed.

My shoes felt a little squashy, but not too bad, and they didn't make any noise or leave any tracks. I went across the room and up the stairs again, and when I was at the top, I rapped on the door, very lightly.

"Dobey?"

For a second I didn't hear anything. Then the chain shook a little.

"Dobey?"

I heard the chain drag. The floors were hardwood, I guessed, or tile, and that chain went from room to room in a big semicircle.

Yes. Laura was *really* good at hiding.

Too good, I thought.

Because I'd never even noticed.

I never noticed that there was a *whole person* she was hiding, and even though I consider myself to be such a hiding expert, she did it so well it was impossible for even me to detect.

So I wondered.

What does she have to hide?

I figured now was my chance to find out.

I raised my hand and put it to the knob. Once again I called Dobey's name, and I don't know how he did it, what with the chain and everything, but he'd sneaked up without making a sound and was right outside the door.

He started to growl.

It was a low rumble, pretty angry-sounding, and I must admit it totally freaked me out.

"Hi, Dobey!" I said in this really chipper voice.

He barked, once, sharply.

I flinched.

"Hey, Dobester!" That's what Laura had always called him. "Remember me?"

Very slowly I turned the knob. I opened the door an inch. I heard his chain shake.

"Hey, Dobey! I'm here! Remember me?" I was still very chipper.

I saw part of his head through the crack. His eye was dull black. I guess it didn't look *too* unfriendly. He was still growling, though.

I put my hand through.

Amazingly, he didn't bite it off.

I won't say he was super excited about me petting him, but he let me. Then he sort of got into it, turning his head all over the place and letting me scratch behind his ears. When he started licking my hand, I opened the door the rest of the way.

At first he backed up and sort of checked me out, and his ears went up a little, I'd say halfway, like maybe he was on half alert, but nothing special.

"Come here, Dobester!" I said, chipper as hell. I put my hand out again. He watched me for a few seconds and then came up, his whole body sort of galumphing straight at me. I must say, my need to pee had returned exponentially. He sniffed my hand, then sort of jolted forward, stuffing his snout in my crotch. I stood pretty stiff and just let him. After a few sniffs and wiggles I guess he remembered me, because he pulled his head out again and let me pat him some more.

I looked around. It was the kitchen like I'd thought, with one of those nifty islands in the middle with stools all around it.

I looked in the corners of the ceiling and saw no cameras. I chalked that up to luck.

Over in the corner by the back door was Dobey's dog dish.

I kept patting his head as I moved toward the dish.

It was on the floor beside a counter. On top of the counter was a bag of dry dog food, and next to that a plastic dispenser full of dog bone treats. As I moved, I bent low, sort of synchronizing all my movements and still petting him, so he'd stay calm. I must admit that when I picked up the treats he got pretty excited.

"Treats, Dobey! *Treats!*" I felt like a moron.

I held the dispenser high and he got *really* excited, jumping up and digging his paws with these big black nails pretty hard into my chest. I kind of walked backwards, staring down at Dobey with an idiotic grin.

"Treats! *TREATS!*"

When I was back at the basement door I tossed the whole dispenser down the steps. The treats exploded all over the place, but I figured ole Dobes would clean up the mess, because sure enough, he charged straight down, his paws slipping and scratching on the stairs, and I shut the door right after him.

CHAPTER

TEN

For a second I just stood there, kind of getting over it.

Then I looked up through the room.

I must admit I was feeling pretty good. That whole trick-Dobey-down-the-stairs-with-the-treats routine, I thought that was pretty clever. That was fast thinking, for me, at least, though I seemed to remember seeing something similar in an old horror movie where the character tricks the demon-dog into going downstairs the same way, which is probably where I got the idea in the first place.

But don't think I was feeling good just because I was clever.

The truth is, I was super excited about being in Laura's house. For the first time in months I felt really close to her. I mean, all my feelings were *reactivated* like I said, and if you've ever really been in love, you'll know exactly what I mean, so just seeing the sink where she might go to get a drink of water or the table where maybe some days she sits and eats her lunch —I mean, I was really excited to see all that.

But first I checked again for video. There wasn't any I could see. At least not in the kitchen. I looked all over the place, the ceiling and walls and even on top of the cabinets, too, to see if anything was peeking down at me, but there was nothing.

There sure was a lot of *other* stuff, though. I mean, Laura's mom—or maybe her dad, who knows—really loved appliances. Because they had every sort of appliance you can possibly imagine.

For one thing they had this great dishwasher, which was the first thing that caught my eye. It was right under the sink counter, sort of built in, and it had this nifty glass front so you could actually see *inside* while the water squirted everywhere.

You'll probably think I'm lying, but the truth is, we've never had a dishwasher. I mean at my house.

Well, actually, we did have one.

It was *me.*

It was *always* me.

I don't know why, but my dad and mom, they thought it was somehow good for my soul or something if I spent a half hour every night washing all the dishes by hand.

So you can imagine how much I wanted a real dishwasher, and this one would have been the best. One Christmas I even asked Santa Claus to bring me a dishwasher. I was, like, thirteen at the time and didn't even believe in Santa Claus, but I thought my parents might think it was cute, my asking and leaving a note and all that, but it didn't work at all. I think it just pissed them off, and all I got was this stupid video game console I've never even played with.

I was happy to see Laura had such a good dishwasher, a really *fabulous* one, and she didn't have to wash all those dishes by hand, although when she saw in my house one day that I didn't have one, I must admit she made some pretty cutting comments about my family's, you know, financial status that made me feel pretty bad.

But now I understood those comments a little better. I mean, if I had a dishwasher like *this,* I too would probably be a bit shocked to meet somebody who'd never had one at *all.*

Everything in Laura's kitchen was like that. New and the best. The island table I talked about was, like, three inches thick of granite or something. The cabinets all had these sliding drawers that sort of rolled out on these casters, making everything easy to grab. The huge fridge had four doors —*four* doors—and was full of organic everything; Laura had certainly told the truth about that.

My mom likes organic too. I mean she likes it *theoretically.* She likes it, and then she buys what's on sale.

The floor was some kind of tile with little pictures of birds in it, and it looked really pretty.

And everything was incredibly neat.

Everything was in *perfect* order.

I couldn't help thinking again of my kitchen, because I swear to god, it's pretty rough. I mean, it's not like it looks like a *bomb* went off in it or anything, but most of the stuff came from my grandmother's house and is, like, at least fifty years old, and some of the stuff, the table we have and the rickety chairs, they once belonged to my *great*-grandmother. And so every time I go into the kitchen it is like my mind is literally *clouded* with my heritage, walking through a collection of musty heirlooms until I feel like I live in a mausoleum, for god sakes, like just when I walk in every morning I'm *bombarded* with the past.

But it wasn't like that in Laura's kitchen at all. It was all just perfect, with none of what you might call the *psychology* of the past just bombing you, and after checking everything out I stepped back in front of the basement door, thinking and looking around.

The door to another room was about ten feet away, just beyond the table. The door was open, but I couldn't see much of the room.

I listened for a while to be sure I was alone. And then, just for paranoia's sake, I checked the ceiling again for cameras, but there was nothing.

So walking really quietly I went over to the doorway and, moving super slow, peeked into the next room.

Wow.

It was a dining room.

At least I think it was a dining room.

To tell you the absolute truth, I'd never really seen a dining room like that before. Well, maybe in a hotel or museum.

The giveaway was the table, of course. It was long and black and mirrored everything in the room, especially this range of windows in the wall, which shone off the table like it was made of glass. And there were these glass things on the table that looked like frozen splashes of water; they caught the light and sort of threw this crazy dazzle everywhere in the room, and these crazy lights hanging over the table looked like they were made of metal coils.

I must admit I was awestruck. I really wondered if I'd even be able to eat my *dinner* in this room. I didn't know if I'd be able to *digest* anything; I thought I'd be too excited.

It was all just so untouched and perfect, and there were these nifty abstract paintings on the walls. I remembered Laura saying how her mom loved to collect stuff like that. One day when we were over at my house, upstairs making out, she told me all about it. We were lying there on my bed and we started talking about art, because Laura said she wanted to go to art school—she'd told me that a bunch of times—and she said that when she went to college she wanted to study to be an interior designer, and now I understood why, after seeing how perfect her house was.

I looked around the ceiling, but to tell the truth, with all that dazzle of light reflected off the table and those glass sculpture thingies, it was pretty hard to spot anything and not just be sort of hypnotized.

But I looked hard, and bingo.

Up in the far corner I saw something, a little dish attached to the ceiling, the same bone-white color as the paint, and it had on it a little blinking red light.

I stepped back into the kitchen.

It might not have been a camera. It didn't much look like one.

Of course, you can't be too sure about that, because a camera can really look like anything, especially a sneaky surveillance camera that you aren't even supposed to notice.

So I felt I couldn't risk it.

There was another door, not too far from the one I'd peeked through. It was shut. I thought it was a closet. There was also a back door, leading out to a deck; I could see some of that through a window. But I knew I couldn't open the back door and go outside because of the alarm.

I went to the shut door and opened it just a fraction of an inch.

It wasn't a closet.

I looked through the crack, and I saw a long hallway with a hardwood floor and a thin red carpet leading all the way to what I thought was the front door. I saw archways along the left wall opening to other rooms, but I couldn't see inside the rooms at all. The hall was empty except for these glass stands with several levels. Some had old books on them arranged very neatly. Others had these little figurines, kind of like the splashy glass things — or I suppose they were crystal — on the dining room table. I didn't see any photos.

I stepped back again, but I left the door open an inch.

I knew this was the only exit. There was just no other way.

But what I didn't say was that there was another one of those cameras — or possible cameras — on the ceiling up by the front door, just over it. I couldn't actually *see* it — it was too far away and the same color as the paint, just like in the dining room. But I saw a red light blinking every few seconds.

If it was a smoke detector it didn't matter.

But what if it wasn't?

The big thing about hiding — I mean about hiding when everybody can see you — is to just blend into the surroundings. A lot of that has to do with how you dress, how you hold yourself, and the sorts of gestures you make.

You don't want to be too sharp with anything. Just be dull.

I mean just sort of play it nowhere, and unless the people around you are trained by the FBI, they won't have a clue that you're there.

Of course, on video you might not get away with that. You just might need a disguise. I mean to really blend in.

If there really was some guy in an office somewhere actually monitoring these cameras — and I suspected maybe there was—then more precautions were in order. I needed a disguise. I figured this was necessary even if the guy was hardly paying attention, which I did sort of have to factor in, because sitting around in an office with your eyes glued to a video monitor must be the most boring job in the world.

So I looked around the kitchen. I was thinking about the red carpet out there.

Scratch that.

Actually I was thinking about a gorilla.

I don't mean a gorilla somehow popped into my head—I mean this *video* with a gorilla *in* it, that really is the best hiding video in the world. It's this video on YouTube, and if you ever want to learn to hide, you've just got to watch it.

I don't know who made it. I think it was probably made by a bunch of top-notch behavioral psychology types at MIT, or maybe Stanford. Anyways, it tells you at first in this title that you're going to be seeing a bunch of guys playing basketball, and you have to count how many baskets they make.

No, how many *passes* they make.

There are two teams, you see, and one's dressed in black jerseys, and the other is in white, I think. And I can't remember whether you're supposed to count the guys playing or just how many passes they make, but if you pay really close attention, you come up with a number like eleven—eleven players or eleven baskets or passes, one or the other—and then a title comes up and says something like "The answer's eleven—did you get it?" And you nod and sort of smile and say yes, you did, and you're really thinking that this whole video was totally pointless and stupid and made by a bunch of total morons who had no other ambition but to waste your time, until another title comes up that asks you something like "Did you see the gorilla?"

And the point is that you never did.

Now, I know that because I just told you about it, the first thing you'll do if you go on YouTube and look this up—which you can find just by entering "gorilla/basketball," I think—is that you'll of course now just look for the gorilla and the whole thing will seem obvious and totally stupid. But had I *not* told you *anything,* you wouldn't have seen the gorilla in a million years, though of course now if you go look it up all you'll do is *wait* for the gorilla to arrive and not count the passes at all.

And let me tell you, it's not just some gorilla way in the background who peeks out behind a wall or something. It's this guy in a *gorilla suit,* and about thirty seconds into this video he sort of shuffles out and turns and looks right at you and even bangs his chest—literally *bangs his chest* right at you for god sakes—and you never even *knew* he was there. It's a *complete* surprise, because what these guys at MIT or Stanford know is that if you pay attention solely to one thing, all your attention is sort of hogged by it, and you won't notice something else that in retrospect looks so blatant and obvious that you feel like an idiot for not having seen it.

And these MIT guys—or maybe it was Stanford, and if it was, I wouldn't be surprised if Jack worked on the video or was even in it, because like Laura said, he's a Stanford man and very involved with what goes on there. Laura always told me that Jack was very, *very* involved, even though I don't really think old Jack was bright enough to have actually thought up the video, or even to have been the guy in the gorilla suit, but was probably, most likely, one of the jocky guys making the passes. Anyway, these guys brilliantly demonstrate one of the best ways of hiding, which is to make the person you're hiding from completely interested in something other than *you*.

I swear, I could have made that video.

I could have even been *in* it.

I bet I'd have made a great gorilla.

I dug in the lower cabinets to see what I could find, and pretty soon I came up with this red towel. I won't say it was the exact same red as the carpet out there, but it was close enough, considering the cheesy color reproduction on most video monitors, because I figured the security system monitors I had to beat would be no better than the sort I'd seen in convenience stores, and they always looked pretty fuzzy.

Actually it was a tablecloth, a sort of vinyl picnic tablecloth that Laura's family must use when they had dinner out on the deck, because I saw a long redwood table out there and a big chromium barbecue grill that looked like a spaceship, and I figured they had dinner out there a lot, or at least as much as possible, so as never to mar the perfection of the incredible dining room by actually eating dinner in it.

What I did now was unwrap this tablecloth—it was zippered in this sort of plastic bag—and unfold it, and then put it over my face and shoulders, so it hung straight down in front of me, all the way to the floor.

That was it.

That was my big disguise.

If anybody saw me—I mean any guy in an office downtown watching a monitor while he was half-asleep—all he would see as soon as I came onto the screen was a sort of big red rectangle moving slowly up the red carpet, and he wouldn't notice it at all.

At least that was the plan.

I went back to the door, reached for the knob, and pulled it open just far enough for me to slip through.

CHAPTER

ELEVEN

I must admit that while all this was going on I was sort of thinking a lot about my dad—I mean, even as I was walking across the carpet down the hallway.

I was going very slow, holding the tablecloth straight out in front of me, stretched pretty tight between both my hands, and taking just one short step after the next.

I figured the less motion I made the better, and I was super careful about not hitting the tablecloth with my knees as I raised them, so I wouldn't, like, *dent* the cloth and make it easier to see.

But even while I was doing all that—and also looking behind myself once in a while, to make sure my shadow was in line with the carpet, because light was coming in from the window on the front door, and the shadow of the tablecloth was like a big rectangle behind me — I had this *nagging* thought in my mind about my dad, because as you know, I'd left the house pretty late the night before, and since I wasn't there in the morning, he might have wondered if I ever came back.

Of course, it wasn't that bad a problem.

I mean, I knew I'd probably get away with it.

I'd been hanging around the house all summer with him, and it's not like he ever really paid much attention to me. He felt too bad about what had happened with my mom, and mostly lay on the sofa watching TV, like I already told you everything about.

The only real problem would be if my *mom* showed up.

That would be hairy.

She still came by sometimes — well, practically every other day — because she hadn't exactly packed up all her stuff when she left, but rather just sort of stormed out the front door and walked the two miles to her mom's house over there in Greenway Terrace.

She'd come around every couple days, and because she refused to talk with my dad, she'd come up to my room and sort of look around and cry about how much she loved me and how sorry she was about leaving, which always made me feel pretty miserable, and then she'd grab something from the bathroom like her styling iron or toothbrush, and without saying too much to my dad, who was always sacked out on the couch anyway and not really up for much conversation, she'd sort of tramp out the door again.

Most of the time her visits were fairly undramatic, but if she were to come by and see I wasn't there and he didn't know where I went, I knew she'd totally blow her top, because one of the things she was always on him about was that he never kept enough of an eye on me.

The truth is, my dad was sort of out of it—well, actually *completely* out of it—and had been all summer since my mom left him. I mean, he might not have even *noticed* I was gone; it wasn't like he spent a lot of time checking up on me anymore. And it wasn't like I'd missed having breakfast with him or anything, because we no longer did that sort of stuff. In fact, we didn't really do too much at all together, at least no family-type stuff, because with my mom gone he just wasn't up to it, because like he said, he no longer had much *vital* energy.

I really felt pretty bad for him and wished I could help him, because when my mom left he just felt he'd lost everything, and of course because of what was going on with Laura, that was certainly a feeling I could relate to. I felt it was really my job to sort of incentify him, if you get what I mean, and sort of get him psyched again about his life and back on his feet and everything. A couple times I even made suggestions to him about a few dad-son experiences, like we should go out to the movies or maybe go to the zoo, which I hadn't been to since I was a little kid. But he was never up for anything and just went on watching TV.

I guess the truth is, I felt it was *my* fault that my dad had just sort of given up on everything, and I really wanted to do something about it, even though they always tell you not to think you're the one responsible for your parents' problems, which, however, is something you might not exactly be able to believe if you were me living in my house in the weeks after my mom left.

I know I haven't said too much about *why* my mom left. And I don't really think it's good to just sort of come right out with it, because it was very personal and hurt my dad a lot, and her, too, and they feel very uncomfortable around each other now — I guess you can see that.

But the big reason she left — the one I think I can tell you about — was really because of *me*.

My mom, I will admit, was sort of always riding my dad about various mistakes he'd made with my upbringing. At least, this is the stuff she always brought up when she was really angry, and also that my dad did not actually care about the family in any way that seemed real, even if he *felt* he cared, because my life — what with me not being too good in school, and not really having a lot of friends, and not having done a lot of extracurricular stuff like a lot of kids do at their parents' behest to sort of investigate their potential, if you know what I mean — well, my mom sort of *blamed* my dad for everything

145

and always said I had a lot of *problems* fitting in because my dad hadn't, you know, sort of provided me with much of an example.

His argument was that just earning a living and paying the bills was hard enough. But she'd get him there, too. Because the truth is, my dad had never really *found* himself when it came to all of that. He *tried* a lot of things, like selling real estate and opening a couple businesses, but nothing ever really clicked for him, and even though I always had new socks and something to eat, it wasn't like we had a lot of *expendable* income, if you get what I mean. But my mom would sort of go to work on him for that every once in a while, for his not ever, you know, having *amounted* to anything, although I will say she forgave him for it, as really any girl should if she knows her husband or boyfriend really, *really* loves her and just can't otherwise make much sense out of what he should do with his life. And she'd yell about what her dad had said—my grandpa, I mean, who died a few months after I was born—about how he felt she could have done *better* than with my dad, because my grandpa, he always said my dad wasn't good enough for her, and that she deserved a better life than he could give her, even though he did get her out of Greenway Terrace. He'd been in the army, Grandpa, and was pretty tough-minded, so I've heard. I won't say my mom *agreed* with what Grandpa said, because she went ahead and married my dad and they had me and everything, but the truth is, she'd bring it all up every once in a while, when my dad had made her mad, just to sort of *remind* him of what she'd sacrificed so as to be with him.

But those weren't the problems that made her leave.

I never found out the real reason.

All I know is that finally there was this *big thing* that my dad did to me, or rather *didn't* do, that really ticked my mom off, and which she left him for. And I never could find out what the big thing was — it had always stayed a mystery to me. And even though I spent plenty of time listening through the floor, I never learned what it was. All I know is that my mom would get, like, super emotional about it, and cry and scream and even throw things.

I was already about a third of the way down the hall, and I stopped for a second to rest my arms. Holding up the table-cloth hurt like hell after a while, especially my shoulders. So what I did was sort of very slowly move my elbows down to my waist, sort of bending them in, so I could just stand there and rest a few seconds. The window on the front door was bright with sunlight. I saw the square of it like it was practically burning through the tablecloth right in front of my face, but all around me everywhere else there was just the white shape of the walls and ceiling all blended together and sort of formless, and the whole house was so quiet and still I could hear cars outside a block away.

Of course, I guess my mom was always right—I mean about how I have problems fitting in.

Actually, I think I have just *one* problem, but it's such a big one that it sort of *includes* just about every other problem you could ever possibly think of.

And even though it's probably the most boring thing in the universe to think about, I really should probably tell you what it is.

So here's my problem:

I don't have a clue.

I started moving again very slowly. My shoulders felt sort of better. I swear, how quiet everything was had sort of started to bother me. Suddenly, all I wanted to do was get to one of the archways. I slowly raised my elbows without hitting the tablecloth, and then I went forward, one step at a time, headed for the closest arch.

I don't fit in, and I can't just *act* like I fit in, because I'm no good at doing all that stuff Carol does, all those lies and everything. And I'm not saying everybody *lies* just like Carol, but what I *am* saying is that a lot of people sort of put on an act anyway, without having to go to those drastic lengths that Carol does for his little "private satisfactions."

In my neighborhood you get *bombarded* by your neighbors' *attitudes.* I mean, it's like everybody in my neighborhood acts like they know *everything,* and can do *anything,* and are, like,

148

totally *competent*. And if you don't feel that way about yourself and don't know how to fake it, you're in trouble.

You get judged if you don't go to the best school or if everybody knows your parents don't have much money despite how hard they try to hide it or if you can't, like, renovate your house every year and sort of really keep up.

After a while, all the people who can do that stuff—and believe me, most of them can—kind of catch on that you're not fixed as well as them and they sort of start to judge you in a million sly little ways. So you have to learn to *behave* in a certain way just to be sort of *tolerated*. I mean, you have to learn how not to draw too much *attention* to yourself. You have to act like you're hiding.

But you know what's funny?

After spending my *whole* life growing up here, I've decided that the competent act all the neighbors have, it's like hiding too.

I mean, the *whole* neighborhood is like a hiding place, where people get seen as something *here*—because everybody knows proof positive that they do all that stuff: send their kids to the right school and keep up appearances and everything. But they're not the same in *other* places, because the few times I've seen parents from Ivy Hill at the beach —and that's only, like, a couple hundred miles away—they always look lost and really pulled out of their shell and *nothing* like how they look in the neighborhood, where they look so totally together.

Maybe everybody in the *world* is hiding in a very important way that I can only sort of partly understand.

But I see it.

I even saw it in the hall as I crept along, very slowly now, because the archway was getting closer. I saw it in how Laura's mom seemed to everybody like this perfect mom who had great habits and undoubtedly felt great about herself and never clueless, and Laura's dad, too, in how he was seen as such a terrific businessman and everything. But after I'd heard how Laura's mom talked, god knows *how* she actually felt about herself, because she was, like, the most clueless and nasty person on earth, in my opinion, and so was Laura's dad, treating his daughter like the invisible girl. Maybe they both felt lost and *completely* clueless but were just super good at putting on an act that fooled everybody.

When it comes to my neighborhood, that's the kind of hiding I mean.

I hope you don't feel it's weird that I think like this, but to tell the truth, living where I live sort of *makes* me think this way. You can learn a lot in my neighborhood, especially if, like me, you're always *watching* and not *participating* the same as when you see everybody swimming in a pool whom you couldn't see if you were actually *in* the water with them and splashing around trying to stay afloat.

And all that watching, that's just another kind of hiding, maybe the most effective kind.

I paused a second and stood there thinking that one day I'd probably come out of hiding.

Maybe when I was twenty-five.

I'd always *wanted* to come out of hiding.

I figured I'd throw a party to celebrate coming out of hiding.

I just didn't know if I'd really go to the party.

CHAPTER
TWELVE

I got to the archway when I was halfway down the hall. I felt lucky because it opened into a room where not only the lights were out but the curtains were drawn. So super fast, thinking that the quicker I moved the less chance anybody watching would notice, I crossed over the bare floor and darted through the archway into the darkness.

Except I hadn't noticed two steps leading down from the archway. As soon as I was through I lost my footing and fell with a *wham* right on my ass.

I hit the floor but managed not to yell, and as fast as I could I scrambled behind this big fanback chair, one of three arranged in front of a big sofa. I just crouched there a minute and held my breath. I felt very tingly, not just because I'd hit the floor, but because I really did expect a siren to go off any second and whirling lights to flash on.

After a few seconds I knew the coast was clear, so I got on my knees and peeked over the chair back, looking around very carefully.

It was a huge room, and wide open, with sofas arranged in this semicircular pattern, little metal-and-glass tables everywhere, and big art books on wall shelves.

Up in the far corner of the ceiling on my left was another little doohickey with a red blinking light.

I knew I had to be cautious. But I figured the room was so dark that I might be able to get away with just walking around, especially if I did it ninja style and sort of mimicked the shapes of things I moved past, like these black sculpture things in the corners and this huge painting on the wall that was all black and white and looked like Chinese writing, which I could pose myself in front of like some of the writing as I passed it and probably not get noticed.

But then again maybe not, and I certainly wasn't up for such calisthenic antics, especially after falling down the stairs.

About twenty-five feet away I saw another room behind a wide entryway. It was almost completely darkened, except for some blue glow from what I thought must be computers.

I began to push the fanback chair very gently, using it like a shield between me and the blinking red light. It slid nicely over the floor, very smoothly, actually. And as I pushed it I looked out over the room, seeing all this incredibly expensive black ebony furniture—I supposed it was ebony just because it was black—and all these artworks arranged on these black shelves that just seemed to float in front of the walls.

I must admit that creeping around in there I felt really nervous, almost like I was scared somebody might just appear from nowhere and jump out at me any second.

But then again, I was sure the house was empty.

Dobey was downstairs, and there was no possible chance anybody would jump out, because even if I did get spotted by surveillance cameras, whoever came to get me would come in through the front door or the back door, and it would not really be a surprise, because I'd hear them and still have time to get away.

So I was pretty sure that I really *wasn't* afraid anybody would sort of jump out at me.

It had to be something *else* making me nervous, and I just sort of paused awhile and looked around, looking over the furniture and the paintings on the walls, trying to figure it out so I could relax and get going again.

Then I kind of guessed what it was.

This will sound crazy, but I mean it was almost like the house *itself* was making me nervous, which I couldn't understand, because I really thought it was fantastic and, like, the best house I'd ever seen.

But I have to be honest with you even if it sounds nuts.

The house was great—but something was *missing*.

Now, I don't want to sound too full of, like, judgments, but I felt something was sort of *absent* from the house, and it really did make me feel so *nervous* I almost felt sick.

I just kept looking at all this stuff around me, stuff that cost thousands of dollars and didn't even look like anybody ever really *used* it—I mean like they hardly ever even *sat* in the chairs or on the sofas, and the paintings just sort of hung there all perfect and untouched, and I doubted anybody really *cared* about them at all.

In a way, it seemed like a house that *nobody* lived in, or maybe *anybody* lived in, because there just wasn't anything about the actual people who lived there.

I mean, for how great it was, the whole house really felt sort of *dead*.

There was just something so weird and *impersonal* about it, and I guess I just wasn't used to that, because my house was such a mess, and nothing *but* personal—*too* personal.

Of course, it's not like I can't sort of see *behind* what I was feeling.

I mean, maybe I just sort of *resented* them having a huge house full of such great stuff that I'll never have in a million years, unless I win the lottery or, you know, accomplish something important.

Maybe I *was* a little, like, sick with resentment.

In my neighborhood that's not too hard to feel, believe me, because if you've heard anything I've said you'll kind of understand that a lot of my neighbors sort of resent what other people have and they don't. And when you've lived around people like that your whole life, it's pretty hard not to act just like them.

But to be perfectly honest, I really wasn't *feeling* resentment or anything—but just this *weird* feeling that the house was somehow off-kilter in some odd way I couldn't yet understand.

To tell you the truth, all summer I'd been feeling pretty weird.

I'm not saying it was Laura leaving me that did it, but everything had begun to feel so *difficult*. I noticed sometimes I had to sort of *control* myself; I worried sometimes that if I just let myself go I might do *anything*, that life might just sort of slip away from me.

I don't mean I was *dangerous* or about ready to sort of lose it, but I felt something had changed in me, because growing up *watching* everything like I said, I certainly noticed other people having more than me and it had never really bothered me—but maybe now it *did*.

I'd sort of *adjusted* to being the kid who didn't have anything. I mean, you can really sort of adjust to that, being just a watcher like I said, like a player without a piece. I guess that was my way of fitting in.

But maybe it was wrong to adjust like that.

Maybe I *was* angry.

Maybe I was sort of *angry* about that, because I didn't know how to change it, and I didn't want to just go on being that year after year.

That wasn't fair.

I don't mean I was going crazy.

And I don't mean I wanted to get *angry* or *hurt* anybody —please don't think that. I mean, I'd hate for you to think that I'd sneaked into Laura's house with some, you know, buried impulse to do something crazy.

But I didn't know.

All this nervousness I felt, maybe I was just sort of worried or scared of what I was seeing. I mean, maybe I'd come into Laura's house just to find out all this stuff about her—to sort of discover for myself that her life wasn't nearly as great as she'd claimed—so I could maybe get over her and not have to love her anymore.

It's almost like I didn't even know who I *was* anymore.

I mean, it was weird, not just the usual at-the-brink sort of feeling you get when you meet somebody new, or are going to a new school and it's the first day, or start at some new job and feel awkward around everybody or something, like it was for me when I first got this job I'd had making deliveries for a pharmacy and had to sort of wait and see if everybody liked me and if I could get along enough to go on working there.

Maybe it was because I'd really stepped over.

I mean, I was doing something I'd never done before, and it really scared me, scared me so much I felt sick, and I worried, you know, about what I might do if I didn't keep a handle on myself.

Of course, it could have just been the house.

I was still behind the chair, and I moved it very slowly. I tried to keep it along the wall so it wouldn't seem too weirdly placed if somebody somewhere checked a monitor. I mean, I couldn't just push it out to the middle of the floor. And once in a while I'd just stop and wait and listen, and look back over my shoulder at the big darkened room, at the blue glowing lights.

That day in my house when Laura had come over—the same day she noticed I don't have a dishwasher and got sort of freaked out by it, which was also the same day she told me all about how her mom collected all this modern art stuff and fancy furniture—that day had actually begun really great.

Laura had said something to me then that I didn't really know how to take—I mean, after she said the thing about the dishwasher, which sort of humiliated me.

What she'd said was, *"I love your house."*

Now, one thing you have to know is that when she said this we were both wearing lipstick.

What I mean is that she'd put some lipstick on me, not because I asked her to, but the thing is, she rarely wore any makeup at all, but that day she had lipstick on, this very pretty dark red color that looked unbelievably sexy, and I asked her what it was like, I mean what it felt like to wear it. That interested me a lot, because the few occasions when she had it on, I'd noticed it hid her face behind a sort of sexy disguise.

So she said, "Put some on and you'll find out."

I guess she wanted me to look sexy too.

We were already in my bedroom, and she sort of gave me this look that made me kind of shiver, and she took her little lipstick out of the purse she had, took the cap off, and then carefully painted my lips with it.

Then she said, "How's it feel?"

Her face was about two inches from mine.

I couldn't stand it anymore, so I kissed her.

I guess having the lipstick on kind of wowed me, because it was like I was trying to swallow her head. When I took a break I saw lipstick all over her face and even on her nose and eyelids and ears.

I was lying there—we were on my bed like I said, and I was practically on *top* of her, panting my head off—and she was kissing me back with these really sticky, gluey kisses that just sort of felt incredible. And it was the first time I ever thought that maybe she liked me so much, *loved* me so much, that she wanted to actually go all the way with me.

I mean, she wasn't really letting me *do* anything, and every time my hand strayed to a place it shouldn't she sort of whacked it away. But this time it seemed more from reflex than anything else, because from the way her eyes were and from the way she lay there just *squeezed* to me, I could tell she really was as excited as me.

And then, I don't know why—maybe it was to sort of break the moment, because things were really only going one way—she looked up and around my room and said, "*I love your house.*"

I guess I should have been prepared for it. Because coming in, after we'd said hi to my mom downstairs, we went through the hall, and every time she'd pass something of mine my mom had tacked to the wall, Laura would stop and say, "Did you do this?" or "Is this a picture *you* drew?"

I must admit I was embarrassed as hell, especially after my mom came over and both of them praised my artwork like I was Picasso or something, which was totally ridiculous, because at least five of the drawings Laura saw, and this weird clumpy clay thing I made that was supposed to be an elephant, dated back all the way to third grade.

So at the moment she said it I just couldn't help but think she was making fun of me. I mean, she always *bragged* about her house, which she'd never even let me *see,* and my house was, well, if you want to know exactly what it was like, it was like one of those sort of cheap antique knickknack stores you find on little roads out in the county somewhere. I mean it had that same sort of cluttered *atmosphere.* Of all the houses around, mine was the king of too-much-stuff-not-enough-room, and everywhere in it—but especially the hallway leading from the front door—was like a *menagerie* of junk from the past sixty years. Everything we had came from my grandmother or great-grandmother, and so the inescapable deduction everybody would make was that we never really threw anything away, because it always was something that *reminded* us of whoever first owned it, and my mom and dad just thought it was way too sad to chuck any of that stuff. So we lived around literal *heaps* of it.

I must admit that what Laura said sort of broke my mood, if you know what I mean.

I lifted up on my elbows a bit and looked into her eyes.

"Why?" I asked.

"I just love it. I hate my house. It's so empty."

She looked into my eyes and smiled. "I like all the stuff you have," she said. She seemed so incredibly innocent and truthful when she said it too, not her usual self, which could be quite hard.

"I don't get it. My house is a dump."

She was still looking at me, with her eyes—and I told you how liquid and beautiful her eyes were—just glued to mine. And she said, very softly, "It's all about you."

For a second that made me think.

Oh, I thought. It occurred to me she meant my artwork, all the dopey stuff my mom had put on the walls.

"You mean my drawings? God, I wish my mom would tear them down."

"No," she said. "Don't ever do that. She *loves* you. You're so lucky to have that. You can't take it for granted."

I suddenly laughed right in her face.

And that was stupid.

Her face changed. Her eyes flared.

Her whole *body* tightened; you can always feel that sort of thing.

Suddenly, she changed the subject and went off on her mom's art collection. She talked about the artists and how much it all cost, or was worth now, and it was, like, millions. She sat up and started talking, almost yelling, about how she was going to go to art school and study art history and interior design.

She seemed to hate me all of a sudden, because she started harping on what I wanted to *do* with my life, and I must admit that I'm sort of like my dad and don't have any idea, and she said that was totally idiotic. "Finding out what you want to do is the *single most important thing* in your life!" she yelled. "You're a *fool* not to find out as *quickly* as possible! Your *whole future* depends on it! *I* think about it *all the time!* Do *you*? Do *you*? Don't you *want* a future? How can *you* be with *me* and not think about the future? What do we have? *Nothing!* You better wake up and *think* about it!"

I swear, she sounded just like her mom, though I didn't

know it at the time. But it was more than that, because her mom had just sounded angry, but Laura sounded *tortured* by what she said, and under so much pressure she couldn't help but scream.

She was so pissed at me that I felt I'd been electrocuted. I saw all this fury in her eyes. I almost wanted to cry. I said, "I just want you, Laura. I'm so sorry I laughed."

She winced at that.

I just curled up on the bed. She'd pulled away from me. I put my fists between my knees and lay there.

What she'd said actually hurt.

I don't think she understood how much.

How could she?

She had her life all figured out.

She was obviously at a great school and was great at gymnastics and had tons of friends. She was rich. She got everything she wanted.

She didn't know it, but what she'd yelled at me was something I'd struggled with my whole life.

I mean knowing what to do.

Because I didn't.

I never had.

I was just like my dad, but I never complained like he did. I never even talked about it.

But I don't really blame him.

I think it is more my own fault.

Because like I said, I don't have a clue.

And even though I'd *watched* people in the neighborhood all my life, I never had decided what *I* wanted to do. I know they say that if you want opportunity you have to make it yourself. I really agree with that. It's just that I'm not so great at seeing just how to *make* opportunities. I just don't know how to *participate*. I'd *like* to participate, I know how *valuable* that is, and I know the neighborhood was made by a lot of people who did nothing *but* participate and they made the houses that sort of stare at you and the streets and everything, and they even made all the rules that nobody understands.

I've never really felt *allowed* to participate.

Maybe I've always felt left out.

Growing up like I did, there was a lot to tell me that I was just a sort of total *nobody* and really just a completely lame loser, and since there's no point worrying about a lame loser's future, I never gave it much thought.

But the truth is that all along I've felt in myself something more important than that, something in me that's really *better* than that, even though it'd take a long time for me to get anybody to *agree* with me, probably because people don't actually *see* me, or see any real *value* in me, which was probably the best reason I ever had to just start hiding *all* the time.

Laura had seen value in me, I guess, when she saw me at the party. But lying on my bed I thought I'd wrecked that.

I felt like telling Laura all this. She was sitting up on the bed and sort of trembling with anger, and I really did sort of want to tell her, but I guess I felt afraid.

So I didn't say a word.

I just lay there.

But I really wanted to *explain* to her *exactly* who I was and everything, but the truth is, I just wasn't sure, except that I knew I wasn't just a lame loser.

And I wanted to explain to her that after a while—if you don't know *how* to participate because really you're not *allowed*, and all you do is just sort of stand around and watch everybody *else* participate—all you wind up with is *yourself*. So maybe you sort of start to *refuse* to participate, because you don't want to mess with that. You *refuse* to mess with that because it's all you've ever had and all you can ever trust, and refusing is the only way you know how to protect yourself.

But I thought she'd think I was selfish and crazy, or had really just left myself out on purpose, or maybe I was just lazy and stupid, so I kept quiet and didn't say a word.

Lying there all scrunched up with my fists between my knees—I mean after what she'd said—I felt like such a total loser, I didn't say a thing. I felt like I had nothing and never would, and she had everything, and I had no idea why she wanted to even be sitting on my loser's bed, like what could she possibly *gain* from it, because she was a total winner, and I wondered why, instead of wasting time with me, she wasn't out *winning* something and being *told* she was a total winner, instead of just sitting on my bed mad as hell at me because she thought I'd made fun of her. But I didn't say anything or try to explain anything about why I wasn't doing anything, because what I *was* doing was trying to hang on to myself—I mean literally just *survive* hanging on to myself. But I knew she'd think that was totally stupid, so I just kept my fists between my knees.

By this time she wasn't even on my bed anymore. She'd gotten up, and a second later she bolted out to the bathroom down the hall to wash the lipstick off her face.

I just lay there.

I felt destroyed.

I regretted everything I'd said.

I was a fool for laughing.

Because let me tell you, if I'd understood her, I bet we would have gone all the way.

Maybe we would have gotten married, for god sakes.

I'd be *married* to her now, I bet.

I'd have done it, too.

Married her, I mean.

But I blew it.

Then and forever.

Because of all the times we talked, this was about the *only* time she'd ever let her guard down and given me a chance to see the real her. She had given me a chance to understand her; she bared her feelings, admitting that she liked my house more than her own, which I could tell was a really, really big thing for her to say.

I got it now, crouching behind a chair in one of her grand living rooms.

She liked the mess.

She liked how it was all about the people living there.

Because her house wasn't like that at all.

I stopped pushing the chair a second and looked through the dimness of the huge room.

This house was perfect.

But it said nothing about the people.

Sure, it said something, I guess, about her mom's interest in modern art, but that's about it, unless you want to add that it said something about how much money they had, because it said that in spades.

But it said *nothing* about Laura.

If I had a house with Laura, it would be all about Laura.

It would be a Laura museum.

I'd have so many pictures of her she'd want to throw them out; she'd get tired of looking at herself. She'd understand why I'd laughed.

But I hadn't even seen a picture of her.

Not one.

I wish I'd listened to her. She was trying to let me get to know her. And now when I think back, that would have been even better than going all the way.

I would have *preferred* to listen, now that I had some, you know, perspective.

But I blew it.

I wouldn't even listen.

I just felt embarrassed and laughed at her. I didn't even try to understand.

I got to the next room; I'd pushed that chair all the way across the floor. I looked in and saw it was a den.

She'd mentioned that.

The den.

It had everything; I'm sure you already guessed that.

Lots of video screens. Lots of things I assumed were games. A bar. A curtained wall that could only be a home theater. Rows of seats.

Boy, they were rich.

I was going in when the front door opened and sunlight flooded the living room through the archway.

CHAPTER
THIRTEEN

 froze.

Whoever was coming in would have to hurry because somewhere off in the kitchen the alarm had started making those sudden loud beeps.

My heart felt like it was stuffed in my mouth.

I heard footsteps go quickly up the hall.

That was my chance.

I darted forward into the den. To hell with video cameras —the room was dark enough.

I couldn't immediately decide where to hide.

The bar.

I slid over to the right side of the room on my hands and knees to where the bar was, dodging between these swivel seats that were everywhere in the shadows. I crept behind the bar, froze again, and listened.

I heard a few more beeps in the kitchen, and the other beeps stopped.

The alarm was disarmed.

That was good.

I felt sweat dripping off me. Up until now it had been all fun and games. I suddenly realized how serious it was.

I was in Laura's house.

It was a major crime.

If anybody caught me, they'd think either I was there to steal or that I was a total creep like Paul Stewart. I'd be arrested and put in jail. Nobody would believe anything I told them. Laura would hate me.

My mind was fumbling.

If I got up and went back into the hallway—which was the only way I knew to get out—I'd get seen. And recognized. They all knew who I was. They'd seen me waiting for Laura those times she wouldn't let me come into her house, and at the play I went to—her school play six months ago—where I met her mom face-to-face.

What the hell could I do?

I kept thinking about it, but I had no plans because I just didn't know who was out there or exactly where they were. If I knew that, I could at least *try* to plan an escape route: either the front door—which would be pretty stupid because god only knows whether neighbors were out in their yards—or better yet, back downstairs and out the window I came in through.

That seemed best, so I had to get to the kitchen.

But I heard some rummaging and banging around in the kitchen, so I didn't move.

Then I heard the person come back out into the hall.

They came up to the head of it, rolling something over the floor. I could tell they went as far as the front door. There was no sound for a second, then a sort of scratching noise.

A motor roared to sudden life.

For a second my heart stopped.

I was sweating all over by this time and damn near crapped my drawers.

But a second later I relaxed.

I suddenly felt cool all over.

I got it.

I almost laughed.

It was a vacuum cleaner.

It was the goddamn *maid*.

I came out from behind the bar on my hands and knees and scrambled up to the entrance to the living room. I looked across the living room toward the hall outside the arches, but I couldn't see much.

I looked up at the camera on the ceiling.

The light still blinked, but I began to doubt it was a camera.

Probably a smoke alarm. And anyways, when the alarm was turned off, maybe the cameras were turned off too.

Maybe.

I had to risk it.

I darted across the living room like a flash, got over to the first archway, and looked through. I still couldn't see much of anything; the angle was bad and just showed me those fancy glass stands with the old books on them.

I moved fast to the second arch, my back skimming against the wall.

There.

I saw her.

It *was* the maid.

I mean the cleaning lady.

She was turned away from me, a small woman in a pale blue knee-length dress, her graying black hair pulled into a bun. She was rolling this fancy vacuum cleaner over the floor, the kind that looks like a droid from *Star Wars* and probably cost a thousand bucks. She was bent over slightly and her head was lowered to check the red carpet as she rolled the vacuum back and forth.

I had to move while her back was still turned, while the vacuum cleaner still roared.

I was so nervous I thought I might puke.

What if she turned around?

What if I tripped or knocked something over, like one of those nifty glass stands?

She'd probably have a heart attack. This poor old lady would drop dead of a heart attack, and it'd be all my fault.

I couldn't stand thinking about it.

So I didn't think about it, but just stepped into the hall — one big long step. I mean, I almost practically *jumped*. The kitchen doorway was, like, twenty-five feet back and full of light.

I spun toward it, and just as I did, the vacuum cleaner went *off*.

I froze dead still.

I was, like, ten feet behind her.

I didn't breathe.

I heard her do something. Maybe pull a piece of carpet out of the vacuum cleaner where it had snagged; there was this little ripping sound.

At my left was a stairwell. I hadn't even seen it as I left the kitchen earlier; I passed right by it because it was sunk into the white wall. It led upstairs, on a curve up over my head.

I still held my breath.

If the maid turned, I was done.

But she didn't turn.

The vacuum cleaner went on again. She started walking

173

jerkily backwards, toward me, always walking backwards so as not to step on where she'd just vacuumed.

I couldn't risk the kitchen anymore. It was too far. I sprang to the left and as quietly as possible ran up the stairs, hoping to god the maid couldn't hear anything over the noise of the vacuum.

At the top of the stairs I jumped to safety and stopped. I dropped flat on the floor and peeked down through a railing.

The hall was straight under me, the front door way up at the end. The maid had come about a third of the way down. She still had her back turned.

I sat up with my back pressed against a wall. I raised my eyes and looked all around. There was a skylight above me. The whole hall was bright with mellow daylight glowing off the pearly white walls.

I saw plenty of windows — windows over roofs.

I could go through any of them, find a tree and climb down. I could pick a place where the roof wasn't very visible through the tree branches outside, and I doubted any neighbors would even notice me.

I thought I'd do that, do it in just a few minutes, once I felt less nervous and got my breath back, because to tell you the truth, I still felt pretty nervous and a little out of breath. If the maid came upstairs, I could just hide anywhere, no problem.

I started to prepare myself for getting out. I even sat forward a little, you know, like I was going to maybe stand up.

But then I sat back again and didn't budge.

Something had sort of *occurred* to me.

Maybe it was because I was just sitting there and had some peace for a minute and could catch my breath and everything, I don't know. Because I started to *think* a little about the whole time I'd been in the house, and mostly about how all my feelings for Laura had been *reactivated*, like I said, and I have to admit that they felt more reactivated than ever, now that I was upstairs and had a second to sort of think and catch my breath.

I mean, up to then I'd really been thinking about how I had to *leave*, and mentally planning all the necessary steps for getting out of there.

But I must admit this thing occurred to me while I sat there, just listening to the maid downstairs, and I completely stopped thinking about leaving.

Because it suddenly occurred to me that I'd come inside the house not really by *accident*.

I was thinking maybe I'd had a *plan* all along, but had kept it hidden, even from myself, because I sort of didn't want to *face* it.

I mean, maybe even coming in the window wasn't, like, so totally *coincidental*, because maybe on one of the million times Laura had made me wait for her when she went inside her house, I'd walked into the yard and noticed that the gardener had this bad habit of running a hose out of the basement window, because he used all the outside faucets for sprinklers, and he left the hose attached to the spigot inside the unlocked window after he'd gone home. And earlier I couldn't really face the fact that maybe I'd sort of *planned* all this in my mind —I mean, sort of *seen* that the window was always left open, and kind of concocted a plan to one day maybe go inside.

But now, sitting there by myself and listening to the maid, I faced it.

My plan, I mean.

I mean, I wasn't really sure I'd done it all on purpose. I mean, I wasn't *positive*. Sometimes, you know, you might do something on purpose, but then keep it a secret and sort of hidden in your mind, and you don't even tell yourself that you actually planned on doing it, because you can't really decide whether it's right or wrong.

I couldn't really decide about that.

But I knew one thing.

I didn't want to leave.

I really didn't want to.

I mean, this was my *one* chance to find out something about Laura. My *only* chance, because I knew I'd never be back inside her house in a million years. I'd come into the house to *find* Laura—I mean to find out something about her that might explain why she left me, and why she ever wanted to go out with me in the first place.

But I hadn't.

I hadn't found out a thing.

All I'd learned was that her life wasn't what I'd thought it was, but that didn't actually *explain* anything. I'd learned that she had seen me, but I still didn't know why, and I still hadn't really seen her.

I sat there for a while and didn't know what to do, really just sat there looking over at the wall across from me, just sort of staring at the wall.

Maybe there *was* something I could find out about her.

I mean, if I stayed inside her house.

I don't mean I wanted to stay *forever*.

No.

For just a *little* longer, until I—

I must admit I felt a little scared.

I don't mean about getting caught.

It really didn't matter if I got caught; that's not what scared me.

For some reason that didn't scare me at all anymore.

I was scared by what I was *thinking*.

You see, I had a crazy *feeling*.

I was here—I knew now—to *do* something.

I wasn't just fooling around being heartbroken anymore.

But what was it I wanted to do? What *was* my plan?

I didn't know.

All I knew was, this was my *one* chance to find out something really important about Laura, like I just said, and I didn't want to blow it.

The truth is, I didn't really know what to feel about Laura anymore.

Because all along, you know, I've had these sorts of *feelings* about her and what she'd done to me—I mean how she'd treated me—and I guess I never really told you, because maybe I was afraid I'd look bad.

But I think I'll tell you now.

I mean, in one way, I guess I felt pretty hurt because she dumped me and really did it just because her mom told her to, at least that's how she *played* it, so she didn't have to take responsibility for hurting me herself, but that wasn't fair to me, because for one thing I was just a sitting duck. I mean, I never really ever had any *leverage* with Laura, if you get what I mean, because when you get right down to it, she had lots more friends than me and was, like, *accepted* by everybody, even idiots like Biff Roberts who invited her to their lousy parties, whereas I didn't have so many friends and mine were all just, like, *fringe* friends as my mom always called them. And so of course I wanted to go out with Laura—going out with a girl like Laura was like a *dream* for me—but I never even had a *chance* with her. And I knew it because she had so much more than me and just always sort of *flaunted* it, and not just stuff but *experience,* too, and I hated it.

I did. I admit that.

I hated it.

I hated that there was *nothing* I could say to make her change her mind when she dumped me—even though I could tell from this terrible look in her face that she maybe actually *loved* me—and *nothing* I could do to show her I had value, because I didn't know how to act and I never had a mask and all I could ever be was myself, and that just wasn't good enough for her.

I just wasn't good enough for her.

I never had been, and I couldn't stand it.

But the worst thing is, I *could* stand it, just like I'd been able to stand living in the neighborhood all my life and just sort of *behaving* so I would be *tolerated.* But this was different.

I mean, the people in my neighborhood never saw me because I was *hiding,* so I didn't care what they thought. It was okay if they thought I was nothing.

But Laura *saw* me.

She saw me, and I wasn't good enough.

I wanted her to love me, but I was *never* good enough for her, and I think she knew it all along.

So why did she want me at all?

There was no reason and no answer, and I was getting no answer snooping in her stupid house.

But I *wanted* an answer.

I refused to leave *without* an answer.

Because maybe if I got an answer for why she just sort of *trifled* with me and hurt me so bad, I'd be satisfied.

Because I was actually really mad at her.

I still loved her—don't get me wrong.

I loved every *molecule* of her.

But I was really, really, *really* mad at her.

Maybe an answer would let me leave her and still love her and maybe forgive her.

But I didn't know if I could forgive her. I didn't know if I *should* forgive her.

All my life I'd sort of trained myself not to *react* to how people treated me and to just let go of how they made me feel, no matter how bad it hurt.

But maybe it was *wrong* not to feel things like that and not get angry and react, and instead just be buried in myself because everybody maybe wanted me to, because it just sort of made me less of a problem for them and somebody they didn't have to see or recognize or care about at all.

Boy, was I feeling weird.

I was really *scared* of myself.

I sat there thinking I'd totally flipped.

Downstairs, the maid shut off the vacuum, put it away, and started doing something else; I couldn't tell just what. She hadn't let Dobey out of the basement yet, but I was sure I'd have his company in a little while.

I thought I had a few minutes.

I got to my feet and quietly stepped through an open door into another room.

A bedroom.

The master bedroom.

Her parents'.

It was fancy like the rest of the house, sure, but I no longer cared about that. I was sick of seeing all their stuff; they had too much of it. But I was glad there was this big window next to the bed, because lots of daylight came through the filmy curtains and flooded the room, making it easy to see everything.

There was a stand on one side of the bed, with lots of drawers. On top was a crystal lamp and a few bracelets in a little box—I figured it was her mom's side of the bed.

I wondered what was in the drawers. Maybe something secret. Maybe something to explain why she was so mean to Laura.

I knelt down and opened the top drawer.

The first thing I saw almost made me laugh.

For all her interest in organics, Laura's mom really didn't have the right to bitch at Laura about eating wrong, because I saw this whole pack of candy bars stuffed in the drawer, huge chocolate caramel nut jobs — you know, the good kind.

I shuffled around in the drawer and found a pill vial.

I picked it up and read the label. It was prescribed for Laura's mom. I dropped it back inside and shut the drawer.

Across the bed was another cabinet just like the first one — nightstand cabinets, I guess they're called. This was obviously Laura's dad's side of the bed.

What was in his top drawer? Maybe it would explain why he acted like Laura didn't exist.

I went over.

When I opened the drawer I froze.

A gun lay there, on a few papers. It was flat and black and had a trigger lock; I'd seen those things in magazines, so I knew just what it was. The whole trigger area was covered in this black plastic blocking device with a weird three-hole key slot.

It just sat there, like — well, I hardly know how to say it — like it was *waiting*.

I wanted to pick it up.

I wanted to get rid of it.

It terrified me.

I didn't know why, but it seemed like a disaster waiting to happen, and I thought I should just stash it somewhere, hidden.

But I didn't.

I reached down urgently to grab it, but my hand stopped.

It just *stopped*.

I just didn't want to *touch* the gun.

I guess it scared me too much.

I felt I was crazy.

You don't have to think that—*I* did.

I *was* crazy.

I reached up under the lip of the drawer. Nobody can hide anything from me. I felt around with my fingers. I touched something held by a magnet and pulled it loose.

A weird key.

It was a round cylinder of plastic with three prongs of stainless steel: three prongs for the slot of the trigger lock.

I looked at the key for a long time.

I put it back, closed the drawer, and stood straight. I looked to one side of the room. There was a master bathroom attached, all marble and silver. I slipped in.

I opened the medicine cabinet.

I stood a few seconds, just looking.

I'd figured it. I used to deliver all this stuff for that pharmacy on my bike.

Lots of vials. All psychiatric stuff.

Laura's mom.

I felt for her. I was such a creep for snooping, but I really felt for her.

I'd lost track of the maid. I listened for her.

There she was, downstairs, going from room to room. She was talking in Spanish on a phone now. She had a pleasant voice. Then she yelled, "Dobey?" With a Spanish accent the name sounded cute, with all the emphasis on the second syllable.

"*Dobey?*"

I heard old Dobes bark from the basement, and the maid's footsteps headed for the kitchen.

I couldn't get that gun out of my head.

I looked back at the nightstand.

It was in there.

It was *waiting*.

All right, I was crazy.

But I wasn't there to hurt anybody.

I'd never hurt anybody in my whole life.

I'd never even *thought* about hurting anybody.

But I already said how all summer everything had begun to feel so *difficult,* and that after Laura left me I had to sort of *control* myself, and I worried that if I just let myself *go* I might do *anything*.

And you hear stories, you know, about crazy people who just go off half-cocked without even *knowing* they wanted to, and I thought about that. I thought about how I'd come into Laura's house and maybe had a sort of plan I didn't really admit to myself, and how I'd come upstairs and looked around without admitting it was something I'd wanted to do all along.

And I'd just poked around in her parents' private stuff without any, like, *compunction* or anything.

I'd hidden so much from myself that I really didn't know what I'd do next.

I mean, what if I *was* some sort of *maniac,* and just not telling myself what I planned to do until I did it?

Because that gun totally freaked me out—I mean I really felt *threatened* by it—but I didn't know why.

I had to leave *now.* I had to get out.

I ran lightly out of the room into the hall, just as I heard the maid let Dobey out into the kitchen, barking happily and smacking that chain around.

Along the wall I saw a number of doors.

I ran silently down the hall through the sunlight coming in from the skylight on the ceiling—very beautiful light.

I came to the last door.

I gently opened it and looked inside.

Laura's room.

CHAPTER
FOURTEEN

I closed the door until it was almost shut.

I stood there right in front of it.

I wanted to go in.

But I didn't go in.

I'd been thinking I was going to *leave*.

But suddenly, I was at her door.

I just stood there like an idiot.

If I went in, it was like I was telling myself I had some sort of crazy *right* to, unless all I really wanted was to just, like, violate her privacy.

I really wondered if I *had* any right to go in.

I thought I didn't, but maybe I was wrong.

I didn't know what to do, so for a minute I just stood there, kind of peeking through the crack but not seeing much, and sort of thinking about whether I had any real *right* to go in, and thinking that maybe, if I believed I'd really loved her, I sort of had *permission,* in a way, to go in—I mean, if I *really* loved her.

But how could I be sure I really loved her?

Maybe I just *thought* I still loved her, but was hiding from myself what I actually felt.

Because I will admit I was pretty mad at her.

So I just stood there and kind of racked my brains, thinking about her, wondering what I really *knew* about her, so I could determine, you know, whether I had any real *right* to go in there, and what I, you know, even really *felt* about her.

But it was really hard to know.

Because I never asked her about herself.

Not really.

I guess I was afraid.

And she never told me about herself.

Not really.

I guess *she* was afraid.

I mean, the truth is, we only had *one* important conversation the whole time we went out.

And I don't mean the time when she said she loved my house, because we didn't actually talk then—she just got mad at me.

I mean *another* time.

This *one* other time.

I shouldn't say we had only *one* important conversation. That's not really what I mean. We talked a lot and discussed our feelings, even for each other, and sometimes it was even quite personal and sort of intimate.

We talked *all* the time, actually—I mean usually about dumb stuff like music and movies and food or whatever, and sometimes about deeper stuff—but only *once* did I have a really, *really* important conversation with her, where I guess she tried to sort of reveal to me who she really was.

I used to think that this was sort of sad or lame or proved we didn't really belong together, because it only happened *one* time.

But when I think about it, most times I talk with people, nothing important gets discussed.

I mean, most people *never* talk about what they really feel, and, honestly, they spend most of their time hoping they'll never have to. I learned that from my parents.

Actually, to tell the truth, me and Laura never really even had any *intention* of talking at all.

I mean, it wasn't like we *decided* to just *open up* to each other and say a bunch of super heavy stuff.

All that happened was, I sort of asked her about a book I'd lent her—well, actually that my mom had lent her—because she'd had it for a while already, like almost a month. She had talked to me about it and said she loved it so much that she'd read it three times. So I figured it was about time she gave it back to me, because my mom had asked about it and was getting impatient.

But it wasn't really the book that was important.

I mean, we *started* to talk because of the book, but talking about the book kind of got me to tell Laura about this crazy stunt I pulled one day, which is what I actually want to tell you about, but sort of can't until I tell you about the book.

But the truth is, I hardly even *feel* like telling you about the book.

First of all, I always found it depressing, and second of all, I never read it.

That's true — I never did.

I will admit my mom told me all about the book. And I read the back *cover.* I read the back cover about a *thousand* times, and it described all about how the girl who wrote the book died, and that just sort of made the whole *theme* of the book a bit too much for me to want to deal with, even though usually I'm a pretty good reader and have read scads of things.

Anyway, I've kind of made a *decision* here, and I hope it doesn't, like, irritate you.

I'm not going to tell you the name of the book.

You see, I think it has a sort of bad influence on people.

The book, I mean.

I'm not saying it shouldn't be in libraries and I'm not saying it shouldn't be read, but what I think — and this is just an *impression* I get, because you remember I haven't actually *read* the damn thing—I think it sort of *glamorizes* unhappiness. I mean, it really *glamorizes* it.

I actually want to tell you the title of the book, and all about the girl who wrote it and what happened to her, but if I do, I know you'll probably just rush right out to read it like everybody else does, and it'll be because of *me*, because I told you. And really, rather than it being because of me, I think I'd rather you just come across the book all by yourself and without my influence, so you can't, like, *blame* me for having told you about it.

Anyways, the book is all about this girl who's afraid of going crazy and killing herself. She's afraid, this girl, that she's trapped in a kind of box. That's not how it starts; I mean, first, of course, you have to read all about her family situation and childhood she couldn't stand and everything, but the thing is, it's like her life is hard—at least *she* thinks it is—while actually it's pretty posh in my opinion, because she goes to this nifty boarding school in Vermont and her parents are loaded, but despite all that, she feels she's stuck in this box.

And the problem is, she can't get the lid up.

I mean, she's always sort of *fantasizing* that she's stuck in this box, which of course is, like, the book's big metaphor, you know, that life is like a box you can't get out of—at least *this* girl can't—and she's so stuck that her only option is knocking herself off, which in the book she *also* fantasizes about and plans in, like, twenty-five different ways.

That's what it's all about.

I mean, that's what my mom told me, and she also told me everything about how the girl who wrote it did herself in, like, literally only a *month* or something after the book was published. So even though I hadn't actually read it, I knew enough to talk about it when Laura and I once took a walk through the neighborhood, just a sort of boring walk, but which turned out to be the *one* single time I ever heard her say anything about herself to try to tell me who she really was.

And I know that now, because I've, like, drawn so much *attention* to it, you're probably thinking that what Laura said *must* have been, like, a really big deal—but maybe it wasn't.

I mean, it isn't like she read off to me her own personal version of, like, the Declaration of Independence or anything, but she said a few things that made a big impression on me, that's all, and I started thinking about that, when I was standing there at the door to her room.

Anyways, we were walking, and I said to her, "Hey, by the way, can I have that book back? My mom said she wants it back. She wants to know if you liked it, though. She asked me."

Laura sort of looked askance a second. It was near sunset, and we were both bored. Actually, *she* was bored, probably because I'd come up with nothing for us to do except take a walk. The day was warm, but kind of *boringly* warm, and the air smelled fresh, but really sort of *boringly* fresh. It *was* really boring, I have to admit it, because sometimes, in *my* neighborhood especially, it really feels like *nothing* is going on and nothing ever *will* go on, and it makes you feel sort of bummed out, just walking past all those staring houses and yards that never change, and I couldn't help but think she might sort of *judge* me for not coming up with anything to do that was more, like, exciting.

"I lost it," she said. She didn't even turn her face to look at me.

Wow, I thought.

I almost stopped walking.

This was bad.

Because this particular copy of the book was my mom's favorite copy. She'd had it since high school and treated it like her own personal testament.

"You *lost* it?"

I was really worried. My mom would be pissed.

"No, maybe not," Laura said. "I just don't know where I put it. I'll look for it." She still didn't look at me.

I could tell something was going on with her, just from how she was walking a little faster and sort of *deliberately* wasn't looking at me. I couldn't really tell if she was *fooling* with me.

To tell you the truth, the feeling I had was that she wanted to *keep* the book, and not give it back to me.

I tell you, that book makes girls act like that.

Then—I think it was to almost sort of change the subject, even though we were still talking about basically the same thing—she asked, "Did *you* read it?"

She said it just like that: *Did* you *read it?* And I could sort of tell already, from this sort of dark attitude I felt coming from her, that she thought I was somebody who'd not *bothered* to read it, and was actually probably, like, the last person who would *ever* read it, given the chance.

"Me? No. I didn't want to. My mom told me about it. She loved it. I don't read that sort of stuff."

"You should read it," she said. She sounded stiff, like a teacher. And finally she looked at me.

"I like science fiction," I said, trying to smile. "Ever read any of that? I like weird stories about different dimen—"

"That stuff's for idiots," she said. "You should read the book."

I walked a bit.

I didn't like the idiot thing.

I didn't feel she'd called *me* an idiot—she hadn't. I mean, she'd said that if I read the book—or at least she *implied* that if I read it—I'd probably get something out of it. I would only have been an idiot if she'd thought reading the book would do me no good at all. Actually it was more complicated than that, but the bottom line was that I could tell she thought that reading it might somehow *improve* my understanding of life, which I didn't believe at all, and which actually kind of pissed me off.

"I don't want to," I said. "I think it might just make me bummed out."

"Then you should get bummed out," she said, and it sounded a bit sarcastic, because she never really said "bummed out" herself, and she had sort of put it in air quotes because it was a phrase I used quite a lot. "I think it would be good for you. I really think you'd *learn* something." She was still looking at me. I mean, her eyes were, like, *glued* to me, like she'd never *stop* looking at me.

"Yes," I said. "Maybe it would." I was trying to sort of half agree so we could maybe discuss something else.

"I'm serious," she said. "You should read it."

"I think I know all about it," I said. I suddenly felt kind of impatient.

"How?"

"I read the back cover," I said.

"Ha!"

I looked at her. "No—I did," I said. "I read the back cover, like, *fifty* times. And my mom told me about it. She told me all about it a *hundred* times, trying to get me to read it. But I don't want to."

"Why not?"

I've got to admit that this was hard for me. I mean, it was so much easier just walking around with Laura, thinking she was a beautiful goddess.

And she *was;* that was the problem.

Actually, for the first time it was sort of *irritating* that she was so incredibly pretty, because it sort of biased me against myself or something. I mean, it made me feel stupid for talking, and even starting to *argue* with her over a dumb book, because the last thing I wanted to do was make her think I was, like, *critical* of her in any way. And I will admit I was afraid that if I spoke the truth about what I felt she might not really like me anymore.

But I couldn't stop.

I really felt impatient.

Super impatient.

To tell you the truth, I was actually getting a little bit *mad* at her, which was weird, because I'd never been mad at her before, and didn't even think I ever could. But for some reason, her just loving this book really pissed me off, and I couldn't help it.

Maybe it was because my mom had, like, *applauded* the book so much to me and I'd never argued with her or told her my true feelings about it.

But with Laura I just let it go.

I let it rip.

I said everything.

I couldn't believe it.

"Yeah, I know what it's about. It's about this girl, right? And there's this thing with her dad—she either hates her dad or loves him and all he does is sort of intimidate her or ignore her or something—and it has the part when she's in boarding school and thinks all her teachers are morons, and when she dreams about being in the stupid box and can't get the lid up, and it has the part that—"

"You haven't even *read* it and you hate it," Laura said.

"I don't *have* to read it! I *live* it! With my mom. I'm sick of it! It's a book that says life is horrible and meaningless, but that's something she has a *choice* to feel or not, okay?"

I was sweating and felt out of breath. I swear, saying all that had been a workout for me. I mean, really, I didn't know what had come over me.

And besides, I was getting this funny *idea*.

I was getting this funny idea that I would tell her something I'd done that she might think was stupid—something I'd never told *anybody*, but I'd tell *her*, because maybe it would make her shut up about the book.

Laura had stopped walking. She looked at the ground, then up ahead, then at me.

"Some people don't have a choice," she said, sort of quietly.

I was surprised. I mean her attitude surprised me, because usually she acted so hard as nails.

"What? To see everything as horrible and meaningless?"

"That's right."

I guess I was kind of mad. I'll admit I was actually very mad at her. She'd really pissed me off. Because I'd kind of put her on a pedestal—and she hadn't exactly *prevented* me, what with all the great stuff she told me about herself—and here she was sort of *deliberately* jumping off the pedestal, saying this depressing stuff, and that really bothered me.

I hardly knew what to think.

For a second I wanted to ask her a question. I wanted to ask, *Do you see everything as horrible and meaningless? Do you believe that BS?* I wanted to ask her all that, because it sort of seemed like what she was saying, without actually saying it.

But it didn't seem possible to me.

She was perfect.

Was *she* unhappy? How in hell? The thought really scared me. Because, I mean, if *she* was unhappy with *her* life, how the hell should *I* feel?

I mean, I know it sounds ridiculous, but up to then, everything I knew about her life was *great*.

I could barely stand hearing her talk to me this way. I wanted to ask, *Why? What possible reason could you have for—*

Instead I said, "There's a choice. There's *always* a choice."

"No, there isn't," she said. "Not for everybody. Because it's like she said in the book. Some people can't stand being themselves. The lid comes down. The lid—"

"Oh, to *hell* with the lid!" I said.

Boy, was I impatient.

I turned and stopped and looked at her. I must have looked crazy, because that *idea* I'd had was sort of buzzing around in my head, and it *felt* crazy. She even looked a little afraid of me.

"Do you want to hear something about somebody not standing being themselves? Something about *me?* Something I never told *anybody?* Do you want to *hear* it?"

"Yes," she said, her voice still quiet. "I would."

"You might think it's stupid."

"I won't think it's stupid."

"You promise?"

"Yes."

"Okay. Then I'll tell you."

We walked along the street, and we went up to my old elementary school, and telling her took the whole time, and it was almost dark by the time I was done.

And she didn't say anything.

She didn't interrupt me even *once.*

She just listened, and she didn't even react at all when I was talking, but just sort of stared ahead and nodded every once in a while, so I could tell she was still listening.

Now, where this thing I told her starts is with Carol. But of course I didn't have to, like, *explain* much about him to her, because her school was like his school's sister school or something, and they'd gone to the same parties and, like, school-related events a lot, so she already knew him pretty well.

I won't say she exactly *liked* him. We'd talked about him once or twice; she told me she had no patience for that sort of snoopy attitude of his, and all those sorts of irritating questions he always asked people to sort of figure things out about them.

Anyways, what I told her about first were Carol's "private satisfactions."

I had to explain all that.

I mean, I had to explain how he sometimes lied about who he was to strangers, just to sort of impress them and see how they'd react, which she thought was idiotic and just another reason to think Carol was sort of a nut.

But what I told her was that I'd actually *talked* to Carol about this habit of his, because it really *interested* me.

At first I worried that bringing it up might embarrass him. But Carol wasn't shy or embarrassed about it at all. Actually, I never once saw him get shy or embarrassed about *anything*. He was really what you might call a sort of pluperfect confident guy, which of course was maybe just an act—because he was, like I said, an actual *actor* in those dopey TV spots—but if it *was* an act, it was the best one I ever saw in my life, because he never let up on it, not even for a second.

But to tell the truth, I didn't just *talk* to him about this habit of his.

What I really did was try to sort of call him to *account* for it; I mean ask him to explain *why* he did it and what was so wrong with his life that he was sort of *addicted* to doing it, but all he did was laugh, and not a regular happy laugh, but one of those dark laughs that basically told me he thought I just didn't have the brains to figure it out. I told him I understood the *respect* thing, and how maybe it helped him fight back against potentially bratty kids who bragged about what they have, and he kind of agreed with that stuff, but he said that really wasn't why he did it.

"It's a *rush*, dude, that's all!" is what he told me. "A total *rush!* I mean, I really can't explain it. You just won't get it unless you try it yourself."

So one day I tried it.

I really did.

I actually did it *myself*, on a day when I cut school a couple years ago.

Now, I don't cut school too often, and I told Laura that, because I knew she wouldn't like hearing that I *ever* cut school, and I hardly ever did. But once in a while there would come a *perfect* opportunity, like if I had a note from my mom saying I had to leave early to go to the dentist or something, and after I was out of the dentist I could just skip the rest of the day if I wanted, and nobody would wonder why I was gone.

Usually I just hung out alone in garages in alleys when I cut school, so as not to get spotted by anybody who might report me to school or to my parents. And that's just how it started on this day I was telling her about. But after a while I got bored with garages, so I figured I'd risk wandering around the streets up there across Roland Avenue, which is this big two-lane street that cuts right through my neighborhood, with all these plants and flowers growing on the median.

When I got across Roland Avenue I went all around, under the trees and past all these big houses built up on these raised yards, so when you walk past them there's, like, a flagstone wall next to you and the yard is level with your face. I didn't worry too much about getting spotted. Nobody knew me up there, and if anybody did see me and wondered why I was out of school, I could just slip away and hide pretty easily.

Now, this whole area across Roland Avenue was what people call the *dollar* side of my neighborhood, where all the doctors and lawyers and big property owners live—the *really* rich ones. Laura knew it was called that; anybody in my neighborhood or any of the nearby neighborhoods would, because that's something you learn no matter where you live around here.

My side of Roland Avenue, where just regular people live, we always call the fifty-cent side. Laura knew that, too. Everybody calls it that. But up there across Roland Avenue, everybody calls it the dollar side. And even though I already told you about The Oaks, where Laura lives, and how everybody over there is rich, you have to remember how I said those are people who sort of come and go and haven't lived there long, whereas these people on the dollar side were even richer, and their houses were the oldest of any around, and the families had lived there the longest.

I walked awhile, just sort of admiring all these huge houses — or really maybe just *trying* to admire them, because I couldn't always see over those flagstone walls as high as my head and felt like I was lost in a huge, hilly maze. I remember the sky was dark with clouds and the air felt pretty heavy and sort of cold, too. Finally I came up to this country club over there, which had these big brown shingle buildings not much different from houses, only bigger, and a big inner courtyard with fenced-in tennis courts, and this golf course out back, down at the bottom of a long hill they let kids sled on in winter-time. I'd sledded there, but I'd never been inside any of the buildings.

I told Laura I probably wouldn't've even *approached* the country club, because I really did think it was completely off-limits. But drizzle started falling and there was no real place for me to stand around outside; I was getting soaked. So I slipped in through this gateway I was passing — they have this big black cast-iron gateway in the middle of this high ivied wall out front — and I crossed the courtyard to this building, where I stood in a doorway. All I wanted was to stay warm and dry, and I was listening to the rain tap on the pavement when a waiter stuck his head out the door, smiled nicely, and asked if I'd like to come in and get dry and maybe have a Coke or something.

I said I would.

He was foreign-sounding, the waiter, with gray in his hair, and wearing this white sort of formal jacket that had brass buttons up the side of the front.

One thing I can say is, he was, like, the politest guy I'd ever met, because he never lost his smile, and he sort of waved me forward with his hand so I'd know exactly where I was going.

He led me into this very fancy and old-fashioned bar area where everything was made of very heavy dark wood, thicker with varnish than a gym floor. There were long tables and big dark leather chairs and sofas everywhere. It was pretty quiet in there, but I noticed a few old men in suits were sitting around, reading newspapers and having drinks.

I sat at the bar and the waiter went behind and poured me a Coke and passed it to me.

And I don't know what it was, but when he asked me some question—just a simple question about where I was from or something—I just went off.

I told him I was the son of the police chief.

I don't even know why I picked that.

I mean, you'd think I'd say I was the son of a congressman or senator or something like that, but what I said was police chief, because it sounded important to me. And I don't mean the *local* police chief, because I sort of instinctively figured they all might know him—the old men in the suits, I mean—so I said the police chief in *Chicago,* because I thought it sounded right, and that I was in town visiting a friend. Then I said—and he hadn't even asked me but I just sort of *volunteered* it—that I went to a boarding school and was on break, and how I wasn't even staying in a hotel or house, but on a big yacht downtown moored at the marina near where the old spice factory used to be.

I kept my eyes on him while I talked; he was polishing some glasses. But the truth is, I wasn't saying all this just to tell the waiter, but more so those old guys—and I'd counted five or six of them sitting around drinking drinks—would hear me.

And sure enough, the more I said about the Great Lakes and anything else I knew about Chicago—calling it the Windy City because I'd heard it called that somewhere—these old guys sort of perked up and nodded and grinned at one another. I could tell they were listening to *everything* I said, until finally—and it only took, like, a minute—they all got up from their tables and stood in a circle around me at the bar while I blabbed on and on.

I don't know what it was, but for the first time in my life it was like I could talk *endlessly.* I'll admit it was a little hard keeping up with all the lies, but I kept track of everything pretty good. I had, like, a lot of vital mental *energy* for some reason, probably because it was a real *rush* like Carol had said, and I could tell that these old guys in the country club had had a few drinks anyway even though it was still morning.

In the beginning I didn't know if they actually believed me, but I just kept talking anyways, because, at first at least, it was really fun.

But the thing is, after just a minute or so, I could tell that none of them were doubting a word I said.

I mean, they *wanted* to believe what I told them—I could tell just looking at their drunk, grinning faces—and if they chimed in and said that at *their* boarding school there had been an indoor pool or polo grounds or some tree everybody carved their initials on—because, you know, they sort of wanted to *relate* to me—I'd say that we had a really big pool and dozens of horses and that an English guy named Withers taught us to ride and play polo. And they never even tried to contradict me, these old guys, and if anything they tried to *encourage* me—I mean even *correct* me—and said my dad was actually police *commissioner* instead of *chief,* because it sounded more official, and so I went along with it, and for a while I was thrilled to be getting all this attention, and I really felt—at least for a minute—that I'd sort of created a new me.

But it wasn't long before something felt off.

I don't mean my lies fell apart; they held together perfectly.

I just for some reason started feeling sort of down.

For one thing, I kept watching these wet, drunk smiles on

all these old-man faces, and their glassy eyes that looked kind of red and teary — and I had the feeling they would never have wanted to know who I *really* was, I mean just a kid from the fifty-cent side.

But as long as I kept it up with the lies, they all were happy and sort of took what I was saying as a chance to relive their own memories, maybe, and sort of *indulge* in their past. But it was like *I* — and I mean the *real* me — wasn't even there at all.

Because all the time I was lying *I* still felt that fifty-cent-side kid inside me. So it wasn't long before I started getting pretty nervous, talking faster and faster, and telling them how I had to leave to get the car that was going to take me to the yacht so I could go watch the nationals, and they asked me *which* nationals — always calling me "young man," which I don't think anybody had *ever* called me — and that confused the hell out of me, because to tell the truth, I don't follow any sport too well. So I wound up saying the *chess* nationals, and told them I was a top-ranked national chess player, and could play blind chess and speed chess and multiples, and I tell you they just ate it up, and the waiter, too, though he looked at me funny sometimes, with a funny smile — a very dignified but sort of funny smile — and he poured those old guys so many drinks, you'd think they'd all have died on the spot.

Then I left and went back outside, and there was no car and no yacht and no nationals.

I hung around in alleys awhile longer.

But I got kind of bored.

I couldn't think of anything else to do that day. So after about fifteen minutes I went back up to Roland Avenue and caught a bus back to school.

I sat on the bus looking out the window, watching the houses pass by.

I thought what I'd done was crazy, except that it was a lot like hiding.

I mean, at the time it felt like the *best* hiding I'd ever done.

What made it different, of course, was that I'd actually *shown* a lot.

It just wasn't *me* I was showing.

I guess I felt pretty bad, because unlike Carol I couldn't just see it as a joke.

I mean, I really felt like *nothing*.

I'd *made* myself feel like nothing by not being *me*.

This was the one time I truly did feel life was horrible and meaningless, because *I'd* made it that way by just throwing away who I really was, like I was nothing.

Now, I've told you all this just like I told Laura. And we were still just walking over the busted sidewalk, but I think we were near my old elementary school by this time. And while I'd told her, I'd sort of gotten excited trying to fit all the details, you know, into what I said, but now I looked at her, and she seemed sort of upset.

"Is that what you are? A kid from the fifty-cent side?"

"Yeah," I said. "What else?"

"Doesn't that bother you?"

"No," I said.

But I thought about that for a while.

I mean, yes, it had bothered me while I was talking to the old men, but on the bus back to school I got used to it.

So I told her that.

"I don't mean I was *happy* with it. But I got used to it," I said. "After a while it didn't bother me anymore. I guess I got over it. I always have."

She still had that look in her eyes. I swear to god she nearly had tears in her eyes. Not tears, but almost. "Doesn't it *scare* you?"

I sort of laughed. "No," I said. "I can live with it. Anyways, I'd rather be me than a bunch of lies."

I looked at her face, tilted downward as we walked, flushed and strained. I don't know what it was, but she seemed in pain. I hadn't meant to hurt her with what I'd said, but I thought maybe I had. Maybe she thought it was just too sad for me to think about myself that way, accept myself that way. I didn't know. I wanted to tell her that it wasn't really so big a problem for me. I mean, I didn't think I'd just be a fifty-cent-side kid *forever*. I had hope, and I wanted to tell her that she should have it too, because from what she'd said about the book, I doubted she did, even though I couldn't yet understand why. I wanted to tell her that I felt I could change my life, and that even if I thought it sucked now, I knew that one day, maybe when I was twenty-five—or maybe even *sooner*—I would take more control of my life, get the apartment I wanted, downtown in some old hotel, and be what I wanted to be, once I figured it all out.

Get my life together the way I wanted it.

Maybe even with her, if I was lucky enough.

But I couldn't admit I wanted her that much. I guess I was afraid. So I didn't say a thing.

We walked a bit in silence. Weirdly enough, she took my hand.

Suddenly, everything felt a bit lighter.

We talked some more.

About other stuff.

Meaningless stuff.

She had this idea about me getting golf lessons, and I'd never even *played* golf, so she said *she'd* give me lessons.

Believe it or not we talked a lot, and she held my hand the whole time.

For one of the first times she seemed sort of *happy* with me. And it was weird, because I'd really kind of *argued* with her—I mean at least when the subject was the book—and not because I'd *wanted* to or even *meant* to, but because I was just so *exasperated* having to hear about that book again that I just had to say what I really felt.

I mean, instead of my usual thing of making her go numb

telling her how beautiful and wonderful she was, I'd sort of *reacted* to her—to what she said about the damn book—and even though she didn't agree with me, she liked it.

I couldn't believe it.

I mean, I'd almost been sort of *mad* with her, almost even *yelled,* because just talking about that book, which I can't frickin' stand, made me feel so damned *emotional,* because I really can't just *accept* anybody telling me life is horrible and meaningless.

But the funny thing is, Laura liked it.

We went behind the school and kissed like crazy. We sat on this jungle gym apparatus, and then when it got darker we kind of crawled *under* the apparatus, and we were really excited and sort of squirming all over the place, and god knows what would have happened, because usually after dark no one's ever back there behind the school, except of course that night somebody came through the dark and actually climbed up the apparatus, some drunk or something, and we had to get out of there.

I know I said I used to talk to Suzie about everything, but that's not really true.

It wasn't like talking to Laura.

I told Suzie everything, sure, but it was all stuff I already knew. Obvious stuff, really. It was simple and easy with her, and we'd feel happy or frustrated, but never in pain. It was just the little facts of my life, parents and school and neighborhood stuff. I never discovered new things that were buried in me or in her, because I never wanted to look for them.

After we talked that day, I felt I understood something about Laura.

There was something deep in her.

And very dark.

She'd wanted to share it with me but didn't know how.

That was big.

Really big.

I think that was love.

And it scared me.

I didn't know if I could handle it.

Maybe we both couldn't, because we broke up a few weeks later.

Anyways, that was the time we talked.

CHAPTER

FIFTEEN

I stayed outside Laura's door a few more seconds, listening.

The maid was still down in the kitchen. I heard the ring of dog food cascading into a dish. Dobey barked, nicely. They seemed to get along really well. She talked to him cheerfully in Spanish. I couldn't understand a word.

Then I stepped into Laura's room slowly and shut the door behind me, quietly.

The room was dark. I couldn't see much yet, only the shapes of the furniture. The curtains were drawn. Vague light bled through, showing the outlines of her bed, a couple bureaus, and a desk with computer stuff on it.

I'd known it was her room because I smelled perfume, faintly.

Flowers and spice.

I'd never asked her what perfume she wore. I wish I had. I loved it. I don't know how to describe it except to say it made my heart race and my mind go blank.

I guess that's a good perfume.

I stood there another minute, listening.

I heard the maid let Dobey outside.

I must have been above the backyard and deck. It was hard to tell, because there were so many rooms in the house. It was easy to get confused. But I heard the door open downstairs, and then I guess she led him out, because I heard her voice still talking to him outside, below the curtained windows. There must have been a chain on the deck to hold him, because I heard the maid drag it across the boards. Dobey thumped around for a minute, and then he must have sat, because I heard nothing more after she came back inside and shut the door.

I still waited, and when I heard her puttering around downstairs it seemed safe to move, so I stepped lightly across the floor and opened one of the curtains halfway, just enough to let in a little light to see by.

Her room was kind of hard to explain.

Laura's room.

It was perfect.

I'd never seen so neat and clean a room in my whole life. I was amazed her mother ever got mad at her. If she'd been my mother, she'd have been on me all the time, because to tell you the truth, I usually made my bed after I got home from school, or even later at night, like right before I got into it.

But not Laura.

Her bed was perfect. It looked like a bed in a fancy hotel and even had one of those throws over it, the kind covered with white cotton pompoms.

I'd always wanted to see her bed. You probably think that's pretty weird. I guess I'd sort of fantasized about it, like I fantasized about whatever else she might do when she was alone.

And here it all was.

But I can't say I liked it.

Not really.

It was too perfect.

Everything was too perfect, too ordered, too organized. I saw that right off the bat. It was just like the rest of the house, like nobody really lived in it.

It made me feel sort of bad. I guess I'd hoped to see a mess.

But I thought, *Hey, it's probably just me.* After all, I grew up in a pretty messy house. I suppose that's what I thought was normal.

Most of everything was white: the curtains and the furniture and the bedding and these billowy things hanging by four corners from the ceiling that looked just like the throw on the bed. In one way the room was simply very pretty and perfect, a lot like Laura herself was always pretty and perfect.

But it didn't *say* anything.

So I was disappointed.

I don't mean in her.

Her room just didn't *explain* anything.

It was like looking at a picture of a very nice girl's bedroom in a furniture catalog, un-lived-in and waiting. I mean, it was full of stuff but seemed empty.

I felt sort of sick. I mean I felt strange just being there. For one thing, I never did really make up my mind about whether I should come in; I mean whether I actually had any *right* to come in, because I knew I really didn't.

I mean, I knew how *wrong* it was, for one thing, what an invasion of privacy and everything. I really was worse than Paul Stewart. I mean, weirdo that he was, he had at least *asked* to come in.

But like I said, this was my one chance to find out who Laura really was.

I just couldn't blow the chance.

It was like I had Tommy Werks standing next to me all over again, looking at me with his weasely little face like I was nuts not to take a chance, and this time I was going to take it.

If there was something in the room that would tell me more about Laura, I was going to find it.

I was going to search.

I didn't want to.

Everything inside me said it was wrong.

It *was* wrong.

I guess I just didn't care.

I went to one of the bureaus resting against a wall. It had a framed mirror on top on a kind of pivot, and some pretty enamel boxes in front of the mirror, painted in a sort of Asian fashion.

I opened them.

Makeup.

Some jewelry.

I closed them one by one.

I opened the first bureau drawer.

Clothes. Tops.

I fingered through them.

Nothing.

I opened the next few drawers.

Clothes, clothes, clothes.

I crouched down and opened the bottom drawer. The second I had it open I wanted to close it. I mean that.

But I couldn't.

I guess all girls have this sort of stuff. Suzie Perkins did. She didn't pack it away so nicely, though, but usually just threw it all over the floor.

The bras were on the left side and the panties on the right.

I swear, I didn't touch them.

Some were cotton; some were fancy lace.

I'd opened the drawer. Why close it?

I knew it didn't matter.

There was no going back on it. I was sorry, but it was done.

Still, it wasn't enough.

You see, I just kept having these *thoughts*.

I mean these really weird thoughts just kept sort of *occurring* to me, like they had out in the hall when I sat against the wall and downstairs and even last night in the basement, and they were thoughts I felt I'd had on my mind all along but was only now letting myself become aware of.

I didn't know how much time I had. I admit I felt pretty scared, because I could still hear the maid downstairs, but not so clearly because the house was insulated pretty well, and I could hear these little thumps. I realized it would be smart to sort of hurry up and get it over with—searching, I mean—so I could find a way out before the maid maybe came upstairs or somebody else arrived.

But I kept having these weird *thoughts*—and *one* thought in particular—maybe just to convince myself to stay there and not be so nervous, because to tell you the truth, I sort of really did want to leave, but I couldn't help thinking this weird thought that there was something *dangerous* in the room, and I really wanted to know what it was.

Of course, maybe it was me.

Maybe the danger was *me*.

Maybe I was losing it.

I stood. I looked around. Her computer was on the desk.

Check her files, her emails? I might be able to ferret out her passwords somewhere in one file or another, or scribbled in one of the notebooks she had stacked on an open shelf in the desk.

But I didn't think it would help.

I knew I wouldn't find what I was searching for—whatever it might be—in her computer.

I stepped lightly to a closet and slid it open.

Dresses on hangers, most of them in protective vinyl slips.

I looked all over. In boxes on upper shelves. In these neat storage containers down below.

Nothing.

I went into every cabinet. The worst I found were the same drugs her mother took.

Mood stabilizers.

She'd never told me.

Suzie Perkins would have told me. She probably would have offered me one. Suzie hid nothing. Had I been searching her room, I'd have learned everything about her in a minute, from what was strewn on the floor.

But here I learned nothing.

Laura's was a good girl's room.

A *perfect* girl's room.

Well behaved and well brought-up. It really did look like a room display in a department store catalog.

I was about to give up.

There was nothing.

Then I found what was under the bed.

When I first felt it I knew I had to be careful. It was heavy. I couldn't get it out without pulling it across the floor. I pulled it slowly and steadily, so the maid wouldn't hear.

It was an open wooden box, about three feet wide and two feet long, the drawer from some old chest.

The first thing I saw were some paintings.

Laura had told me a little about them. I mean she'd mentioned a couple times that she loved painting, when she told me how she wanted to go to art school, which she told me that day we were kissing on my bed. I don't mean she talked *too* much about it, but just sort of mentioned it, because she always said she wasn't good enough. You could kind of see she felt that way. The paintings I found weren't signed on the front or anything, and only when I turned them over did I see her initials on the backs of them, in the corners, small and hidden.

I looked at one. It was a little hard to see because of a reason I'll tell you about in just a second, but I thought the painting was all right.

No, it was better than all right.

It was a picture she must have painted from life, or from a photo, I guess, because it looked pretty realistic. It showed a field in the country with a white fence, one of those fences you always see along the side of the road whenever you drive out far enough, and behind the fence there were three horses, two brown and a gray one, with their heads pressed together over the fence, and in the background there were trees.

Everything was really well painted and proportionate, but that wasn't what made it good. What made it good was the way she did the light, because there was, like, a bar or a stripe of light across the horses' heads, and more light fell onto the field behind them, making certain areas of the grass bright with sunshine, while the rest of the grass was in shadow. And then very far in the background I saw another horse running, buried in shadow.

I really liked the picture.

To tell you the truth, I liked it a lot more than any of her mom's stuff on the walls downstairs, which mostly looked like building materials screwed together, like wall displays for siding in one of those big hardware superstores.

Laura's painting seemed really human. It was crazy that her mom hadn't hung it up on the wall. You could really feel Laura's love of horses, which was something she had never even told me about.

I liked it.

I think I loved it.

It said something about her, I thought. It was sort of serene, but also sort of sad.

The only problem was the X.

That was the problem with all of the paintings, and there were, like, half a dozen of them, all really carefully painted on canvas boards, and all with big Xs gashed into them with a knife or a key or something.

Another painting was of Dobey and I thought it was terrific. He was sitting on the grass, and it looked like a real painting and not just the flat smeary mess you see a lot of times, but again there was the X.

That was hard for me to deal with.

It scared me, actually.

It scared me a lot.

I wanted to look at the other paintings because I could tell they were all good, but they all had the damned Xs, slashed on them like open wounds.

I hated the Xs.

I couldn't stand the Xs.

Her mother had said painting was not practical; I remembered that now. Laura had told me how her mother had said that.

I tried to think clearly about that.

All I could think was, *To hell with what's practical.*

I couldn't look at the paintings anymore. The Xs were hateful.

It was like Laura had attacked her paintings.

It was like she'd attacked herself.

I took them out and put them face-down on the floor beside the box.

What was under them was worse.

There were all these prizes, certificates, and medals on tangled ribbons she'd won since she was a kid—I could tell by the dates. There were at least two dozen of them, lying on a bed of shredded paper. I lifted them carefully and put them aside.

No, it wasn't shredded paper. It was lots of photos of her.

They were all torn up.

I wondered, *Did Laura tear them up?* My mother had done that too—I remembered my grandma telling me. But my mother had only hated how she'd *looked*. I stirred my fingers through the torn shreds and looked down at the paintings I'd turned over to hide the horrible Xs. I closed my eyes.

I said, "You don't hate yourself, Laura."

I did not say it because it was true.

I said it because I hoped it was true.

I took out the pile of torn pieces and spread them on the bed. The pieces all looked similar for some reason, and then I got it. They had all been taken in a gym, and all of them showed her doing gymnastics exercises.

For a second I wondered why she hadn't thrown the pictures away. She'd torn them up—what good were they now? All I could think of was how some kids scar themselves—they cut themselves with a razor or a knife, and they are left with the scars. They like looking at the scars.

These were her scars.

Some of the photos were pretty big—I mean the pieces of them. I managed to put one photograph together like a puzzle;

I found about seventy percent of the pieces. It showed her on the balance beam—one of her legs was missing, but the other one she was sticking out straight in front of her; and part of the background was missing, part of the wall over the rows of those bleachers they have in gyms.

She looked incredible in this white-and-blue leotard. You wouldn't believe the muscles she had.

In the background I saw other girls too, all of them gymnasts in the same leotard—a team leotard, I guessed—standing off to the side in a line, obviously waiting for their turns on the beam. And there was a man standing off to the side of the beam, making a gesture with his hands. From the shape of his mouth you could see he was yelling something to Laura; he was probably her coach. He was a pretty young guy, maybe thirty, and pretty handsome and muscular, with short blond hair. He seemed hard and intense. In the picture Laura's face was totally focused but worried. I could see that. I could see the nervousness through the fixity of her face, mostly in her eyes. I'm not just making that up—I could see it. She was afraid of screwing up. That was obvious.

I really wanted to see the rest of the picture, especially her other leg and the whole complete pose with her arms spread out like wings.

I rummaged my fingers through the rest of the torn pieces and found what I thought would fit. Two of the pieces had these colored rings. I put them together, placed them where the wall was missing over the seats, and stopped, unable to breathe.

It was the Olympics symbol.

I didn't understand.

She had never been in the Olympics.

It was impossible. She'd told me nothing about it, nothing at all.

I sifted through the pieces but didn't assemble any more photos. I couldn't stand to because whenever I found a piece with her face on it, there was always that same look, that hard focus over a look of fear.

One thing remained in the box.

A diary.

I picked it up and put it aside.

I quickly put everything back in the box, and then I took the diary in my hands and sat with my back against the bed, staring across the room.

CHAPTER
SIXTEEN

It was a red clothbound book, one of those classic girl's diaries, with a strap and key lock on it to keep it private. It said *Diary* on it, in gold cursive letters.

I held it, looking at it.

I didn't want to read it.

Anyways, I couldn't open it without the key.

I *wouldn't* open it, even with the key.

I sat there for a while, my back to the bed, and when I got tired of that I lay on the floor and looked at the ceiling. I guessed the maid was gone by now; it must have just been her downstairs day or something. I didn't hear her anymore, but from a couple barks I knew Dobey was still out back on the deck.

I just lay there thinking, the diary still in my hand.

I had all these weird *ideas*.

I don't really know where they came from, but after looking in the box, I just sort of *had* them, and I lay there just trying to add them up.

I didn't want to read her diary—I mean it.

But maybe I wasn't very serious about that, because I started looking around the room again—just sort of looking around—trying to think of where she might have hidden it.

The key, I mean.

Of course, I'd already looked everywhere.

In every box and drawer and everywhere else.

So I just sort of skimmed the room, trying to see if there was any place I'd missed.

And then I laughed because I saw something funny.

My mother's damned book.

It was right there under some papers on Laura's computer desk, on one of the narrow shelf spaces beside where Laura's beautiful legs would be when she was sitting in the swivel chair there, doing her homework or something.

I couldn't see the cover, but I knew I was right just from looking at the way the pages were all worn and stained from being read a million times. I could recognize that.

What was funny is that it was hidden.

I mean, that's what made me laugh.

Even in her *room* she'd hidden it, stuffed there in the papers like it was some kind of crazy secret she didn't want anyone to see.

She knew *I* wouldn't see it, because we'd broken up, and even when we were together there wouldn't have been any chance of my ever spotting it lying around, because she'd never let me come into the house—I told you all about that.

But it was hidden anyways.

I guess it was so private she *had* to hide it.

Maybe she didn't want *anyone* to see it, her mom probably most of all. I kind of had the idea it was something she'd never want her mom to know she had read and liked so much.

I wondered if I should take it and bring it back to my mom. But I knew Laura would notice it was gone, and she wouldn't know who had taken it, and I didn't want her to freak out about finding it missing.

Still, I sort of felt like taking a look at it.

So after a minute I pulled myself across the floor and took it out of the papers.

I looked at the cover.

I turned it around and read the back cover for about the million and first time.

God, what a depressing book.

Of *course* she didn't want her mom to know she liked it. She would never talk about it with her mom, because it was a book about a girl who had nothing but *trouble* with her parents, so what good would it do to talk about it?

But she'd talked about it with me.

Well, she *tried* to.

She *tried* to talk about it with me, and all I did was kind of go off on her, and then tell her that crazy story about the country club, because I guess I just couldn't stand it. I couldn't stand hearing her praise the book and relate to it, and even just *holding* it in my hands made me feel kind of very nervous.

The book really bothered me. I admit it.

I guess it really bothered me to talk about it, even though maybe *everybody* in the whole world can relate to it because maybe sometimes the lid really *does* come down, and maybe I really *should* have read it, because, you know, "everybody in the whole world" I suppose includes me, too, but I'm sorry, I still can't talk about it, and I just don't want to ever read it.

Because I can't accept that.

I mean the thing about the lid.

I mean, maybe the lid's been down on me my *whole* life.

Maybe it's been down on *all* of us our whole lives, but I can't accept that.

I *hate* that.

I mean, if I had a motto, I think it'd be "Ignore the lid."

And even if I haven't exactly lived up to that motto, I've at least done a pretty good job of *pretending* the lid isn't there, because I just can't stand *hearing* about such stuff and actually find it kind of incredibly disturbing.

But Laura didn't mind hearing about it.

She *liked* hearing about it.

She wanted to *talk* about it.

But I sort of didn't let her.

I still had the book in my hand and I hadn't even *moved* in a while, but the funny thing is, I was sweating. It was crazy. I was sweating like I'd run around the block, and I was breathing, too, pretty heavily, and I figured I had to calm down. I mean, I really had to calm down.

Because I must admit, even just *thinking* about the book *still* made me a little mad at Laura. I mean just for ever even bringing the damn thing up, and I wished my mom had never *loaned* it to her, and I wished the lady who wrote it had never written it and had just *thrown* it away; I really couldn't *stand* it. And all Laura ever wanted to do was sort of *shove* it in my face, just like my mom always had, and make me just sort of *hear* all about it and accept *everything* it said.

I couldn't believe I was mad at Laura again, because after seeing her wrecked paintings and all the ripped-up photographs, I felt nothing but *sympathy* for her, knowing what I now knew, because it was just too sad and depressing, and I'd thought I could *never* be mad at her again, and probably hadn't ever *really* been mad but actually just sort of jealous.

But I *was* mad.

I had to calm down.

I mean I really had to sort of *relax*.

I kind of waited a minute.

I waited to calm down.

Of course, I can't just say that Laura had wanted to bother me with it. I mean, I don't think it was, like, her plan to *deliberately* hurt me. I *felt* pretty hurt and it did piss me off a lot.

But then I sort of thought that *if* she didn't want to hurt me —I mean, if that really wasn't her *plan* to sort of just *shove* the thing in my face like my mom always had—maybe she was doing it for some other reason.

Maybe she was trying to tell me something.

Maybe she was like the girl in the book.

Maybe she was trying to tell me that.

But I didn't listen.

It never even *occurred* to me then that she wanted to maybe, like, *share* it with me.

Sharing is something they talk about when you're little, like six. I think it's by the time you're maybe ten that sharing goes out the window.

But she'd meant to share it with *me*, in a way.

I put the book back. I mean I just sort of stuffed it back into the papers where she'd hidden it.

I must admit, I felt pretty stupid.

I wished I'd talked to her about the book.

I wished I'd read it.

I wished I'd had the nerve.

I really bet I *should* have read it.

Because I hadn't shared *anything* with her.

Well, maybe a little.

Maybe something.

But I felt I really didn't deserve to look at the book anymore.

She could keep it.

It was hers.

I thought she'd probably earned it.

I was lying on my back again by now, in the dark. Just a little sunlight from the windows fell in bars across the floor. I was breathing better, sort of relaxed.

The diary was on the floor next to me. I looked at it.

I rolled over to the closest bureau and opened the bottom drawer. I grabbed all her lacy underwear. It felt scratchy in my hands. It was the only place I hadn't looked, the only things I hadn't touched.

Now I touched them.

I lifted them out and there was the key.

I crawled back across the floor, opened the diary, and read it straight through.

It wasn't very long. I mean, just a few hundred pages, and

she'd used up less than half, making entries daily if she'd felt something was important or exciting but usually just weekly, and sometimes less than that.

She'd started it when she was a kid, around ten. That was the first part of it, what I'd call the happy part, the entries printed in big handwriting and dated in the upper corner of the page, like she was writing something for school. I admit I skipped a lot of that, because it was all pretty much the same: happy times with her mom and stuff about gymnastics competitions, with lots of exclamation points after saying how excited she was to be winning a prize or taking a trip somewhere with her parents and Jack.

And then it got darker, I mean after she turned twelve, and there were many fewer entries, less excitement, and fewer exclamation points, too.

It broke off completely when she was turning thirteen but started again when she was fifteen, the handwriting now small and neat, etched across the pages, sort of frantic, with a different kind of excitement, and no exclamation points at all.

But it wasn't just the handwriting that had changed.

It took me an hour to read it, and when I was done, I went back to my favorite occupation of staring at the ceiling.

I never was a kid pressured by his parents to do anything.

I mean *be* anything.

But Laura was.

I don't really understand parents who do that. I mean, I understand wanting your kid to be somebody important and encouraging them to be the best and all that. I mean, in one way I can see how it would be great. There'd be lots of pressure, sure, but you'd get to learn something really well, and that would make it sort of worth it, as long as your parents knew when to let up.

As long as they knew your breaking point.

Laura's life had been all about gymnastics, but she never told me. It was over by the time I met her. All I ever saw her do was a couple flips in the park.

I know I shouldn't tell you this; I know how wrong it is to just sneak into somebody's room and look through all their things and read their diary and everything and completely sort of *expose* them, but you have to know. It's important that you know because then you'll maybe understand.

I guess the one thing I felt bad about was that there was very little about me. There was almost *nothing* about me—I mean at first—and I admit I tried to find what she'd said about me, because I very much wanted to know what she felt and whether I'd really ever meant anything to her at all.

But she said almost nothing.

I met a boy last night. He's very cute. I like him. He's different.

Okay, that was me. And except for a few entries about places we went together, that was about it.

It hurt my ego. I admit it. I loved her so much and she

thought so little about me. It really hurt. All the early entries about me were so simple: *I went to the movies with him. I went to the park with him. Last night Jack drove us to the rink; he can't skate worth a damn.*

Of course, she could barely even say that because of everything else she said, about her mother, about her father, about gymnastics, and how she felt about herself.

At first even *she* didn't know how she felt about herself.

It came slowly.

My life is perfect! she had written. She was ten. *Mommy made me promise her, I will be her perfect girl! She said that when she was a girl, they didn't have what we have. She couldn't follow her dream — her parents took it away! She said that she and Daddy give me everything. Mommy's dream was to be in the Olympics! I can be in the Olympics if I work hard — Mommy said so. It's my dream too!*

Laura trained *all* the time, during the school year, at summer camps, constantly. I did not know a human being could work so hard, and she was just a kid. She practically *lived* at her gym. She skipped food for days at a time to meet weight requirements. She did things that would have driven me nuts.

I will be everything Mommy wants me to be!

In one way I guess she did love it. In a way she was proud. I saw that in the park when she'd do the flips. She loved knowing how to do something so well.

And there were, like, *benefits*.

She'd never told me about her other friends. I think I mentioned that. Well, maybe it was because she didn't have so many anymore.

But she *had* had them. Plenty of them.

At her gym she was part of this elite little crowd, only the best girls—only the winners—and as long as she was a winner, everything was cool.

At school, too.

I mean, it's not hard to imagine how it was, because she was, of course, really pretty and rich, but even more than that, she did great in school because she wanted to be the best in everything. Jack was the best in everything. Even though they had lots of dough, he wound up getting a whole *scholarship*. And her dad's example was, like, sort of incredible. Super achievers, all.

She'd had loads of friends; at school she was like a jewel, a little athletic straight-As princess who—as long as she kept it up—could do no wrong.

I've never had friends like that. When I read about how her life had been, I couldn't understand why she'd ever wanted to know me at all. Thinking she could have ever loved me seemed crazy. Because I don't mean she had fringe friends like I did, hanging around with Carol in an alley somewhere or crashing some rich kid's party, like we sort of had with Biff

Roberts's. I mean friends who you go on ski trips with—and I've never even *been* skiing—or camping in upstate New York, and even trips to Europe and stuff. I mean she walked with an elite crowd. She'd been *popular*. And she knew all the rules: the right girls to know, the right boys to date. Everything.

As long as she kept it up.

I couldn't relate to any of that. To me, being popular would be like trying to solve the most complex math problem imaginable, all the time. But she could manage it pretty well.

Still, her mom was never satisfied. *Mommy says I can be the best and I will be! I'll try harder. She will see how hard I train! I'll do anything to get better! I will be in the Olympics!*

Laura went to competitions, traveling all over the country with her team. Her coach and her mom designed a tough routine to display flawless maneuvers, and she practiced it over and over. At her best, she ranked in the top one hundred in the nation.

But it didn't seem to matter. Her mom said it only proved she wasn't number one.

I can't wait to tell Dad how I did at the finals when he gets back from Europe!

He came back with a necklace, but he didn't give it to her. She had only come in third.

For gifts, she had to be first.

That was the deal. And she wanted to be first. She told

herself it was all she wanted. *Mommy and Daddy say gold is the only color — the only color!*

When she was fourteen she tore a thigh ligament doing a split. She spent a month in bed. She passed her time fooling with a painting set she'd gotten from Jack, painting scenes she remembered from drives and trips she'd taken — stuff that had absolutely nothing to do with gymnastics. She was amazed by how much she enjoyed painting, and just how free she felt exploring her imagination.

And for the first time, she was pretty upset with her mother.

She doesn't care that I hurt myself! She says it's my fault. She won't believe I'm not good enough. But I'm not good enough. Coach says I have limits. I can't get back to where I was. I'm not sure I even want to.

She wrote about talent and instinct and reflexes and being a natural and stuff she thought her mother couldn't understand.

I couldn't understand.

I never faced such stuff.

I had never had to.

She found reasons to avoid the gym, and she felt her father and Jack avoided *her.* She began to hate living in her house — a house she no longer thought she deserved.

I thought back to last night, when I had stood outside that

basement window; I'd imagined living in her house would mean you could breathe, that you'd actually be on *display* in such a house and wouldn't ever need to hide, because your problems would be exciting. But I hadn't understood that being on display meant facing someone else's expectations, and Laura felt herself falling short every day.

Mother says Jack has done so well—why can't I? She yells all the time. "What—are you so special? Does failure make you special? You selfish monster! What gives you the right to turn your back on everything we've given you?"

I understood why she liked the book so much. She must have felt it was her autobiography.

But it didn't give her any answers. At least no good ones.

The box was her life. The lid was shut tight.

She felt inescapably trapped.

Mother says I must try out for the trials; she'll hate me if I don't. I can't. Coach says I don't have the balance. I'm not a natural. I want to do other things. . . . Nothing helps. I'm going to fail.

She quit.

She tried talking to her dad. But he was busy. That hurt even more than her mom's being mean. *He's never had time for me; he just gives me things.* "Do what your mother says" *is all he tells me.*

When Jack was back during winter break he laughed in her face. "*What are you gonna do now, Laurs? Go to loser school?*"

After she stopped doing gymnastics, her teammates didn't want to know her anymore. They thought she was crazy. Mostly they ignored her, except for some nasty comments on social media. Those hurt too. Laura ripped up her photos. *They were* never *my friends.*

Her life was hell.

A hell of expectations and obligations she refused to keep up with anymore. And nothing yet to fill the gap.

I read what she did and how she walked away from her old life, but with no idea of how to go on.

She started hating herself.

And then she met me.

Oh, boy.

I guess she was intrigued that I could be nothing and still walk around. I had no parents driving me on, no heavy friends to keep up with.

Maybe that's why we went out, I thought.

I guess that was my answer I'd wanted so badly.

I can't say I felt very proud of it.

I was the loser she could learn from.

Learn how to stand people thinking she's nothing.

Maybe that's what she saw in me that was more important than whether my family was rich or whether I'd been to the Bahamas. Maybe it helped her a little bit. Maybe that's what she really liked about me and tried to talk to me about—even though I refused to talk—by bringing up the book and my house and all that crap, that I could somehow *stand* being a kid from the fifty-cent side and not worry about being anything else. Maybe she even envied it.

I *did* worry, but she never saw it. I wouldn't let her.

I couldn't really gather my thoughts at first. I just sat there looking around her bedroom.

I'd only seen one other girl's room before in my whole life. Suzie Perkins's.

Boy, was her room different.

It had Suzie Perkins written all over it. I mean, it was like the Suzie Perkins explosion. I don't think she even understood the *concept* of putting anything away.

But Laura was none of that. Here, it was like everything personal had been forbidden, until whatever remained of herself had to be hidden under her bed in a box.

I understood now why I'd thought so much about Suzie when I was in the basement. I mean, for all her problems and lack of money and pressure from her mom and all that stuff, Suzie was *happy*. She felt good most of the time, and even felt good about her mom, who had rules and everything, but never just *dumped* on her about not being *perfect*. Suzie never had to hide from her *real* self like Laura did, so she could live up to expectations. Sure, Suzie had been offended when Carol had done the squeezie thing, and maybe she didn't know what to make of me when I didn't kiss her, but the thing is that she could get over all that and move on to what came next. She was malleable. You know, adaptable. Healthy.

I knew now why I hadn't kissed Suzie. I couldn't have stayed hidden with her. With Suzie I'd have felt everybody looking at me and knowing I was there, because that's what Suzie was all about. She *liked* being seen. I don't think she knew what hiding even was. Suzie was happy for the most part.

Laura wasn't.

I knew that now.

Her suffering was something I'd been totally blind to, because when you get right down to it, I'd only seen myself when I was with her, and only cared about how I felt and whether she loved me and wanted to go all the way, which I'm sorry to say I often did pressure her pretty hard to do sometimes. Well, actually, I pressured her almost *every* time we were alone, and especially those times when she wore something short that showed her bellybutton, because that would almost drive me crazy, because I'm not kidding when I say she had the sexiest bellybutton in the world.

But good for her that she never did, I mean go all the way, because I knew now — well, I think I'd always known, but now I actually *accepted* it — that I didn't deserve her.

I'd never even tried to find out who she really was.

Not that she gave me much of a chance. She tried to, but she didn't really know how.

So I couldn't blame myself too much.

I mean, I was a mess.

So was she, even though I didn't notice at the time.

What do you get when you add one mess to another mess?

A bigger mess — that's simple addition.

I couldn't help her.

Not then.

She'd hidden from *herself.*

Until she was totally lost.

That's the most dangerous kind of hiding. Everybody knows you, but you're not really there, even for yourself.

I'd hidden from the world all my life.

But never from myself.

And even the weird ways she'd treated me, sort of not letting me be around her parents too much, like she thought I was an embarrassment — maybe *she* was embarrassed about what *I* might see. She wouldn't let me in the house and made me wait outside for twenty minutes because she was ashamed I'd see how *she* was treated, not because I wasn't good enough.

She always looked at me like she wanted to see something in me that just wasn't there.

It was love.

I loved what I saw, but not what she hid from me, not what she sort of tried to tell me about when she said she loved my house or wanted to talk about the book. I *couldn't* love what I couldn't see.

Maybe she didn't think the real Laura could ever be loved. I had to know.

There was more about me in the diary, finally.

A whole lot.

There were, like, twenty pages of this very fine small handwriting, like she'd become somehow suddenly obsessed with me and just scribbled like mad.

It began three months ago, around the time I followed her to that funeral. She'd broken up with me the week before that.

I didn't understand why she got so suddenly interested—I mean reinterested.

It really surprised me that she had all these incredible feelings about me, these sudden *incredible* feelings.

She blamed *herself* for my never having seen her, for never opening up to me and letting me get to know her. *I always pushed him away, I was so mean to him, I was so terrible, I never told him my feelings, why didn't I tell him, I made him feel like he was nothing, what happened to him was because of me, he did it because of me, it was my fault, I did it to him, I can't forgive myself, I can't forgive myself, I loved him but I wouldn't let myself feel it, I wasn't allowed to feel it. . . .*

243

It went on and on. I must say she blamed her mom quite a lot.

I was glad to learn she really loved me.

But that wasn't the important thing.

There was something else.

There was a thing I'd done that had changed my life completely and had affected her so deeply she'd decided to do it to herself.

It was something I'd forgotten. But now it came back to me, and I sat there for, like, twenty minutes staring at the ceiling, because I suddenly *knew*.

I knew exactly what had happened to me that had changed her, and even more suddenly I knew exactly the *reason* why I'd come into her house, the *real* reason. I knew it crystal clear as if I'd always known it my whole life.

I could remember everything, too—I mean *everything*— and to tell you the truth, I knew exactly what was going to happen unless I did something to make sure it didn't happen.

And right then—at that *exact* second—I heard the door open downstairs and I knew it was her—it was Laura—and she'd cut school and come home early.

And if you want to know how I knew it, it's because it was all written down and planned out in the diary.

But I somehow knew it anyway because I saw it all in my mind.

I heard her coming up the downstairs hallway.

I froze.

I stayed there and I stared at the windows across from me and I didn't move a muscle, because I knew now that three months ago I'd had an accident, and I had died.

CHAPTER
SEVENTEEN

I heard her walk up the hall and go in the kitchen. She put her book bag down on the table and sat on one of the stools.

I could feel her under me. I could see her sitting there. I could see her staring at the living room door.

After a few minutes she got up and walked back into the hall and turned onto the stairs.

I got up quickly.

I wondered whether she would be able to see me when she came into the room. I was uncertain about that, just as I was uncertain why I could see her as she walked through the house, because when I stopped *trying* to see her, I was just staring at the empty, quiet room.

Still, it wasn't right to just stand there watching her.

I stepped over to where the curtains hung over the windows, beside a partition wall with corkboards on it where she'd pinned some notes and schoolwork stuff. I slipped behind a curtain, pulled it completely shut, and waited, standing very still.

She came up the stairs, but she didn't come into her room.

She crossed the hall to her parents' room and stood outside the door for five minutes.

Then she went in.

She went straight to her father's bedside table, opened the drawer, picked up the gun, took the key from under the lip of the drawer, removed the trigger lock, and dropped it back into the drawer. She put the key back under the lip, closed the drawer, and stepped out into the hall with the gun in her hand.

She came up the hall, opened the door to her room, and entered.

I watched her through the veil of the curtain.

She had on her school uniform: a white shirt, blue necktie, plaid skirt, and saddle shoes. I'd seen her in it before. The girls at her school have to wear all that stuff. They've worn the same sort of uniform for sixty years. Laura hated it.

She shut the door silently and stepped to the center of the room. She gently put the gun on the bed.

She stood still for a moment, her figure just a hazy shadow in the middle of the darkened room, until she sat on the bed, picked up the gun, and pressed the barrel to her left breast, over her heart.

I said, *Laura, stop.*

She stopped.

At first she did nothing. She didn't move. Her face was lowered and her hair had fallen around it.

I stepped out from behind the curtain.

I came forward a step, looking at her.

She raised her face.

Slowly.

She looked at me.

Through me.

I now knew just how good I was at hiding.

She couldn't see me.

I didn't even know if she could *hear* me.

You can't do this, Laura, I said. *Please. You can't do this.*

I was lying. I knew she could.

I saw her face. Her beautiful face covered in shadow: dark, fixed, decided.

Ready to die.

I didn't know where to begin.

I prayed not to say something stupid.

I'd thought of great things to say to her—when I was behind the curtain I'd really thought of great, comforting things.

She had to *listen.*

But everything had just sort of vanished from my mind.

I thought nothing.

I said, *I'm here with you, Laura. I didn't mean to die.*

It was stupid to say that.

I leaned closer.

I died. But I didn't mean to. They think I meant to, but they're wrong. It wasn't your fault like you think. You had nothing to do with it. I just can't ride a skateboard, that's all; I'm really lousy on a skateboard. I got run over by a bus. But it was an accident. Can you hear me? I didn't do it because of you. My dad bought me a skateboard; my mom told him not to, but he did it anyways, and I got killed. That's all.

She stared at me, through me, across the dismal room, as if into a fog. She couldn't see me at all.

Maybe she never had.

I had to *make* her see me, but I didn't know how.

I said, *Laura, listen to me. Try to hear me. Try to see me. Don't do this to yourself. It doesn't matter what happened with gymnastics. Forget your mother. Forget your old friends. You can't believe you are nothing. I don't care if that sounds stupid. Believe me, I know things now. I've seen things. I know your life is bad. I know it hurts. But you can change it. It won't always be this way. You have to believe me.*

She was small, lonely, and afraid. Her face was so full of pain that I couldn't stand it.

I wanted to touch her, but I knew she wouldn't feel me. I wanted to scream, but I knew she wouldn't hear. She didn't hear me at all, and I knew it.

I kept talking anyway. *I've seen what's in the box, Laura. I'm sorry I looked. I love your paintings; they were beautiful. I looked everywhere. I saw everything. I know it's killing you. But it doesn't matter. Not to me. I never loved you for those things, Laura. I love you, Laura. I don't think you're a failure. You were done performing your routine, that's all. You'll do other things. I wish I could tell you what you hope to find, but only you can find it. I hope it will be beautiful, but I just don't know. All I know is that it's your life. It doesn't matter what other people think. To hell with them. It doesn't matter if they don't love you.*

She shivered, her eyes frozen with dismal misery, staring through me into the gloom.

I looked at her.

I tried to finally see who she was.

All I could remember was the moment I'd met her.

The moment she'd woken me to something I'd never imagined could be real.

She'd woken me to love.

And it was wonderful.

But it had hurt me too.

Falling in love doesn't seem possible until it happens. I never believed I could love until I met her. She brought love out of me, and it was something hidden so deep I hadn't even known it was there.

Now all I knew was that I hoped I could do the same for her.

I got on my knees in front of her.

Listen to me, Laura. I know you're in pain. But you'll find other people. You'll find other love. You found me. I loved you. And now that I've seen everything, I love you even more. I'll always love you. You saw something in me that no one else ever saw; I hid it from everybody! You saw that little bit of value I have that lets me be myself. See it in yourself, Laura. But you have to hear me. I can't stop you, and even if I could, it wouldn't work. The time would only come again. You have to do it, Laura. Pull the gun away.

Did she hear me? I didn't know. Her eyes were wet. But she did not pull the gun away.

It was hopeless.

I knew her.

I knew how hard and determined she could be.

I had to tell her everything.

Every reason in the world why she mustn't do this.

But there was nothing more to say.

Every reason I thought of fell apart instantly.

In the face of death, everything was trite and stupid.

I told her *she* had to want to stop, and stop right now. I told her that she could *tell* somebody how she feels, a counselor at school or a doctor, and she had to get help, because she was wonderful and beautiful and worth it.

I know. That was a mistake.

I really didn't mean to say it. I knew it was boring and redundant—my mom had told me—and I'd said it a million times before and it had never done any good.

But I just couldn't stop myself.

I *tried* to think of other things to say.

Really.

I told Laura again that she had to stop and not do it and that everything would be all right and that if she found help she would believe that, because she herself was so much more than anything she could possibly ever do or be for anyone else.

I told her that I knew I'd never been able to help her; that she'd looked to me for help but never found it because I'd never had the courage to really show myself to her, but she had to see me *now*.

I closed my eyes because I was crying, and all I feared was that I'd hear a horrible noise, and I wanted to tear the thing from her hands, but I couldn't—only she could do that.

And so I just started to say it, even though I didn't think it was even the right thing to say, though in my soul I knew it was the *only* thing to say: *You're wonderful, you're beautiful; you're wonderful, you're beautiful.*

I think I said it ten thousand times—*You're wonderful,*

you're beautiful—and I knew it was hopeless, even though I heard her starting to sob.

I couldn't stop her.

I kept saying it over and over like a prayer.

You're wonderful, you're beautiful.

And I closed my eyes and waited for the sound I dreaded hearing, and I slid into a clump on the floor at her feet.

I lay there for longer than I can remember. Until I knew I was alone.

But I guess she heard me.

Because when I opened my eyes, she was gone downstairs, and had left the gun lying on the bed.

I had to go.

My time was up.

I had something else to do, somewhere else I needed to be.

I don't mean to sound strange. But I had the feeling that just after I died I had been somewhere I could not quite remember, and I'd met people who had explained things to me about how my new life would be. But then they sent me back, and they made me believe things were as they'd been before, when I was alive. They took away my memory of the new things I'd seen, so I could see Laura this one last time, to truly see her and say to her the things I knew were true, now, when they were most needed.

I knew I could go there now, back where I had been, and

when I got there I would see the people again and everything would again be clear to me.

But first I went downstairs, and there she was.

She was standing in the living room with her phone in her hand; she'd taken it from her book bag.

She was thinking of who to call.

I looked at her for a moment, hoping it was not the last time I would see her.

I'm going now, I said.

Her face was wet with tears. Her skin was red, her eyes puffy.

She was afraid of what would happen when she told—I could see that—of what they would do to her, where they might put her and for how long. When she finally called her doctor and told him to come get her, she cried convulsively as she explained to him what she had almost done but stopped and not done—because she said she felt it was a *voice in her soul* that had stopped her.

But after she hung up she stopped crying.

Her eyes opened wider with a harder resolution than I had ever seen in them.

In her eyes was strength.

I saw it.

It was a light, and it was small but growing brighter, and I knew that it could never be put out.

I had finally seen her.

I smiled.

She smiled. Her eyes stayed hard, but she smiled, looking with wonder at what she'd never seen before.

She was looking at her true self.

EIGHTEEN

I could have left then, but I stayed.

I mean I hung around the neighborhood awhile.

I'd never really seen how beautiful it all was, all the houses and stuff, and all the trees everywhere.

I guess I felt like seeing all the people again, just one last time, you know what I mean?

I went down the big hill, and I went a bit farther until I got to York Road. I stood on the same corner awhile, right where I'd stood on the day of my funeral, just looking around. The funeral parlor was right across the street. That seemed incredibly appropriate. I mean convenient.

And then, without really looking or even caring to look, I walked into the street. The cars passed through me.

So this is where it had happened.

It seemed incredible.

How could anybody think I had done it on purpose?

I went farther, right to where I had gotten hit. The bus was coming.

I mean, come on.

On *purpose?*

No way.

I was just a klutz on a skateboard, that's all. Didn't anybody *get* it?

The bus came closer. Nobody was at the stop. I stood there and it went right through me, a big ringing metal box. I saw the seats inside, all the handrails, people sitting and standing around reading the paper. It was crazy.

When the bus was past I turned and watched it.

The day it happened, it was that lady cop who found me. She came up first, I mean. She tried, but there was nothing she could do. She cried. She tried to hide it, but she cried, you know?

I sort of liked her after that. I mean, I couldn't actually remember what had happened yet, at least not back then, but I suddenly thought she was pretty nice, and I always wanted to thank her—I mean for just being around and looking out for everybody, because it really proved she wasn't the mean lady cop some of my friends said she was.

So I did. That day in the grocery. Now I knew why she had looked at me so strangely and hadn't said anything.

She couldn't see me.

But she'd smiled. I guess she'd heard something.

The bus was going to the city, downtown. The other way it went up into the county where all the malls are. We went to the movies there, once, Laura and me. We rode the same damn bus.

I couldn't even remember seeing them at my funeral.

I mean all the people who had come.

At the time it was like I couldn't see anybody but Laura; she really sort of absorbed all my attention. I mean, she really had a way of doing that.

But I do now. I can remember *all* the people who had come now.

It was really quite an event. Lots of neighbors, kids from school, parents, you name it. My fourth grade teacher who'd never, ever called on me even once, and that must be some kind of record. Suzie was there and she cried. And her mom, looking rather large and stoic. Carol brought *his* mom, looking sexy, of course. Even Mr. Miller, my next-door neighbor, and I must admit that he's really the *last* person I'd ever expect to have shown up, but he did. I guess my dad invited him.

I talk a lot about hiding, but from the size of the crowd, it seemed like maybe they'd seen me all along.

It occurred to me, something funny—that veil Laura wore. Maybe she wished we'd been married. I guess we had the same wish.

I'll tell you, they really do a great job when they want to fool you. I mean, I don't know if *you* were fooled, but I sure was. I mean, come on. They fake you out like a simulator ride, only better, a whole lot better, just to make it all seem real. I never was hungry — they just put that there. I guess they wanted to see how I'd react, you know, and get their little private satisfactions. I didn't even really ever have to pee; they just threw that in because somebody has a great sense of humor. I still can't decide whether Dobey saw me or not. I guess I still have a lot to learn. Maybe dogs have a sense for this sort of thing. And walking around with the tablecloth over me? Had that tablecloth even been real? I felt like an idiot.

I was given this task for reasons I can't understand.

I won't say I saved her. She had to save herself.

But I put an idea in her mind.

I felt good about that. I mean, I don't want to sound funny, but I felt I'd finally accomplished something pretty important.

Maybe I *asked* to do it.

I mean, I needed to have *something* to do, right? Anything was better than just hanging around my house. I'd spent a whole summer cooped up with my dad, listening to him talk to himself, bemoaning his fate, and even though I *sympathized* with him and everything, it really had become a little tiresome.

I was a *ghost,* for god sakes, just wandering. I had no idea what was going on.

Still, one thing puzzles me.

Maybe I was sort of dead my whole life, because I'd been hiding, and being *really* dead barely mattered, so I didn't even notice until after the end.

Maybe I never even *was* hiding. Maybe I just thought I was, but really I was just reacting to never feeling like I was truly being seen.

But maybe this is not about hiding.

Maybe what this is really about is how I don't think life is horrible and meaningless, even if it sometimes seems to be.

I know I said that big things never happened to me.

Well, that's still true.

Because this happens to everyone.

And you know, you can't say something's *really* big if it happens to everyone.

It'll happen to you too.

At the right time.

Because like my mom said, there's a right time for everything.

I mean, sure, she said that when I was complaining about sex, but doesn't the same advice apply to everything?

You have to show yourself.

You have to let people know you are there.

You can't play hide-and-seek with your life, no matter how safe it may seem. You'll get too good at it after a while, just like I did and Laura did, and you won't be able to tell anybody where you are or how to find you.

You know, I never told you my name.

I was Danny Preston.

Don't ever hide.

ACKNOWLEDGMENTS

A number of wonderful and beautiful people helped me write this book. I want to thank my wife, Alma, for her suggestions, encouragement, and support—but mostly for her love. I want to thank my son, Hugo, for his love and encouragement, and for proving every day that a boy can be his own perfect self without ever having to hide. Alma and Hugo, you are forever the most wonderful and beautiful people in my life.

I want to thank my agent, Dan Lazar of Writers House, for his constant support, and for bringing my work to Clarion Books, and to my editor, the fabulous Anne Hoppe. Anne, your encouragement and faith in my writing led me to look deep enough into myself to find this story, and your sensitive comments and suggestions—through all the various drafts—helped put in my hand a light I could shine on Danny and Laura, to bring them out of hiding and into the brilliancy of their true selves.